SUBURBAN HUSTLER

ROBIN BOREN

WWW.MARTINSISTERSPUBLISHING.COM

Published by

Martin Sisters Books, a division of Martin Sisters Publishing, LLC

www.martinsisterspublishing.com

Copyright © 2011 by Robin Boren

The unauthorized reproduction or distribution of this copyrighted work is illegal. Criminal copyright infringement, including infringement without monetary gain, is investigated by the Federal Bureau of Investigation and is punishable by up to 5 (five) years in federal prison and a fine of $250,000.

Names, characters and incidents depicted in this book are products of the author's imagination or are used fictitiously. Any resemblance to actual events, locales, organizations, or persons, living or dead, is entirely coincidental and beyond the intent of the author or publisher.

No part of this book may be reproduced or transmitted in any form or by any means, electronic or mechanical, including photocopying, recording, or by any information storage and retrieval system, without permission in writing from the publisher.

All rights reserved. Published in the United States by Martin Sisters Books, an imprint of Martin Sisters Publishing, LLC, Kentucky.

ISBN: 978-1-937273-07-01

Fiction/Thriller
Editor Brittani Wolanin

Printed in the United States of America
Martin Sisters Publishing, LLC

DEDICATION

To my family, thank you all for the love and support through the years.

Fiction/Thriller

CHAPTER ONE

In this life I have been compared to a lot of things, but none of them were closer to my heart than being compared to the Joneses. I spent most of my childhood trying to keep up with all the rich kids in my class. They would come in with a new shirt or pants from the name brand stores in the mall while I was lucky to get a clearance item from Wal-Mart.

I never could understand how those kids got anything they wanted, while I had to beg for even the simplest little thing. If I had only known then what I know now; I could have saved myself a world of misery and grief. I convinced myself when I was in high school that I would not grow up poor. I decided that I would go to college and make a life for myself and never look back. So while all my friends were out partying and having fun, I was at home studying and researching scholarships. There wasn't an event I didn't try out for or a sport I didn't play, just trying to be the best so a scout would discover me and I could get that free ride. Of course as my luck goes, I didn't qualify for any scholarships and I definitely wasn't any good at sports, so I took the working route.

I met my husband Chris while I was going to community college and working at a local tavern. I worked most nights and he would come in with all his fancy college buddies and they would laugh and talk about all the dreams they had for the future. I would feel his eyes on me every time I walked by. He would smile at me and always left a substantial tip.

One day he finally worked up the courage to ask me on a date. There was no way I could say no, because as he asked he snorted and beer shot straight out of his nose and down the side of my arm. He was so embarrassed, but didn't flinch until I said yes. We had a great time that night and I knew then that he was the one and have we been together ever since.

Our life at the beginning was very hard and there were days I knew for sure we would fail and end up having to move in with my parents. He had big dreams of owning his own trucking company, but had a hard time starting at the bottom. I guess he assumed since he had gone to such a prestigious college he would automatically become a millionaire. Once he came back to reality, he went to work at the best trucking company in the city and decided he would work there until he saved up enough to have his own and our lives would start from there.

I, of course, stayed at home and took care of the household and tried to make a name for us. I became involved in the community as much as possible. I started my own little Avon Company and went door-to-door selling make up and becoming friendly with the neighbors. We lived in a nice blue-collar house with all the trimmings. We spent the weekend mostly outside, taking morning walks and stopping to talk to everyone. Chris's goal was to make connections, he knew that everyone in the neighborhood was a part of some inner circle and he wanted to be in the dead center. We would plan great big barbecues and invite everyone we knew. It took me weeks to prepare for them. It seemed to me that I would have to start planning for the next one the day after the one we just had. Chris made his way up the ladder at the company with rapid speed. He knew what he wanted and knew exactly what it took to get it. We were the model couple, happily married and in love. We had the best neighbors and the best friends. We were the couple everyone wanted to be and for a while I was satisfied with that, but not for long. I told Chris one day that I wanted to go back and finish my business degree so when he opened his company, I could help him out. He explained to me that as soon as we got on our own we would start a family and I would not have any time to work because I would be at home taking care of the children. I should have been happy with that and gone on with our little charade, but I felt incomplete. I needed more than Mrs. Wilson. I wanted a life all to myself.

The first several years went by in a haze. I felt like I was sitting on the sidelines watching Chris make all his dreams come true. He was amazing, working and socializing, and knowing exactly which move to make at the exact moment it should be made. I had never met anyone like him and I was fascinated. He was a nirvana for the times. Anyone who met him instantly fell for his charm. Even the bosses at the company he worked for spent more time consulting with him, than actually being in charge. There was no doubt in my mind that my husband could rule the world if he wanted to. I on the other hand spent most of time trying to keep up. I felt I was lacking in being the infamous wife of Mr. Chris Wilson and that was when it hit me. I took a long hard look at who I was and what had happened to my dreams. I had spent years trying not to end up poor and if the day ever came that Chris didn't want to be with me; well I would end right where I didn't want to be.

I decided to take matters into my own hands. I joined the local YMCA and took some self-defense classes. I also took up sewing and baking classes. I swear I don't think there is anything they won't teach you there. I told Chris about my classes and he loved it. What he didn't know was that a couple of the classes I told him I was taking were actually courses at the local college to complete my degree. I had managed to complete all but about 4 classes, so it wasn't hard to hide those in with everything else. So there I was a self-made woman and my husband was none the wiser. I finally made it to my graduation day and there was no one to share in the celebration because there was no one I could tell. If I told my parents they wouldn't agree with keeping it from Chris, and everyone else I knew was through him. I had what I needed to finally hold my own with my husband and it felt wonderful.

CHAPTER TWO

Once he decided to take the leap and venture out on his own, the bosses who once loved him turned their backs on him. He must have seen it coming from a mile way, because he never skipped a beat. A lot of the customers that worked with the old company now came to be with Chris. He agreed that I could run the office for a while until he could find someone that he trusted enough to take my place. That was the last I ever heard of that. I spent my days wooing customers and taking potential clients out for lunch. I spent my evenings at home taking care of the house and entertaining all his friends. My husband was unstoppable, he had everyone eating out of the palm of his hand and never suspecting a thing.

One day as I was entering the office, I saw something I will never forget. There was a strange car parked outside and it looked like it had been there for quite some time. I stopped and stared at it for a while, but just shrugged it off. I never even second-guessed that car would signify the end of life as I knew it. I walked in and sat in my chair and began my daily routine. I started the coffee for the drivers, then I set out the usual breakfast and bathing items. Chris said when we first started to set up the office there had to be

9

showers and plenty of cleaning items for those drivers that spent most of their time on the road. As he learned in his years as a driver, finding a descent shower is not easy. At least they could get good and clean here. We had finally made it and we were living comfortably now. It seemed like this day would never come, but it did and I was extremely happy. My husband was on top and running the most successful trucking company in the state. I was of course right by his side and doing exactly what a loving wife does.

I got home later that night and Chris was already there waiting for me. He had a gorgeous dinner on the table (ordered out obviously). He greeted me at the door with fresh flowers and a jewelry box. He escorted me to the table, pulled my chair out, and placed my napkin in my lap after I was seated. I wasn't sure what he had done, but I was going to get to the bottom of it. He sat down across from me and told me to open the box. I opened it and saw the most beautiful necklace inside, but was shocked when I read what it said. Mother, what was I going to do with a necklace that said mother? He grew the biggest smile and reached for my hand. He told me that he was ready for a family, and he hoped that we could start trying as soon as possible. I didn't know how exactly to respond. I mean, I did want to have children, quite a few children to be frank, but it was too soon for me. As I looked over at him and saw the look on his face, there was no way I could deny his request. So I nodded my head and he leaped out of his chair, scooped me up in his arms and kissed me like he hadn't in a long time. We sat and had a wonderful meal full of discussion about our day and I couldn't help but think that all of this would soon end. That there would be days we wouldn't even have time to sit down together and eat. When we were done, he of course led me straight upstairs to the bedroom. He proceeded to tell me not to bother with the birth control, because it wasn't needed any more.

***

The next few months were touch and go. I began to see a side of my husband that I had never seen before. Chris was use to snapping his fingers and getting exactly what he wanted, but for some reason this time we just couldn't get pregnant. He went to a doctor and was checked out with great health no reason he wouldn't be able to conceive. That just left me, the barren one I was the reason we were having problems getting pregnant. There was something wrong with my female organs and it would be a miracle for us to be able to have a child. I spoke to my husband about adoption, but he of course would not hear of it, we were going to have a child of our own one way or another. We spent several hours and thousands of dollars going to this specialist and that one trying to find a way for us to get pregnant and it ended in sadness every time. We tried In-vitro several times, until it finally worked.

We were about 3 months along in the pregnancy when I started to bleed profusely. I had a miscarriage and my husband was devastated. He wouldn't even look at me for several days after. We spent weeks in an awkward silence. When I came in a room, he left. If I was at the shop he was working from home. Finally one day I came to him and asked him why he blamed me, why he hated me? What he said to that was not what I expected he would say. He proceeded to tell me that he didn't blame me at all, that it was in fact his fault for putting my body through so much that it wasn't ready for and as he watched me go through all the pain and misery to satisfy his needs, he knew that I was more willing to make him happy then he was to make me happy. He laid his head in my lap and began to apologize for being so selfish. Never, in all the years that I've known this man, have I ever heard him apologize for anything. We sat there together for quite a while just holding on to each other and being in love, which of course led us straight into making love.

Now as I am sure you have heard several times before, you can't actually get pregnant until you've stopped trying. About three weeks after that night we spent together I went to the doctor to get some antibiotics for the flu I couldn't shake and he then told me that I did not have the flu, but simply, that I was pregnant. Chris was so scared that he put me on complete bed rest. He hired a nurse to come and stay with me during the day while he was at work. I wasn't allowed to do anything. I had my laptop to keep up with payroll and book keeping for the company, but anything other than that was strictly off limits. There was no way I was going to be able to handle this for another nine months, but I knew for Chris's sake, I better keep up appearances for him.

As time went on I became friends with the nurse and we made out our own arrangement. She did the heavy lifting, but I handled all the rest and agreed that I would take a nap in the afternoon to get my rest. So my pregnancy was quite nice, I had such support from all my friends and especially my husband. All my late night cravings for exotic food were taken care of in a heartbeat. He rubbed my feet and even put on my shoes when I got too big to see my feet. He told me how pretty I was even when I was as big as a house, he was perfect. When the delivery day came, it was around noon and I had laid down for my afternoon nap. I woke up in a pool of liquid and freaked out. I screamed for the nurse and she came in and knew right away what was wrong. She told me to get up and get dressed because we needed to get to the hospital. She called Chris and told him to meet us there. She grabbed my overnight bag and called the doctor to let him know that we were on the way. This lady was a pro, so levelheaded, no wonder Chris picked her. We made our way to the hospital and after several hours of labor we finally had the most beautiful baby boy I had ever seen.

Thomas Daniel Wilson, my son he was simply amazing. He was well worth all the torture I went through being pregnant with him. I vowed the moment I saw him that there would never come a day we wouldn't be together. Our joyous day also brought great sadness when the doctor explained that I would not stop bleeding so they had to go in and do a complete hysterectomy, which in short meant no more children. Although neither of us really seemed to mind. Chris had a strapping son who would end up to be just like his father. I on the other hand had a son who would be a momma's boy, and I would spoil him rotten. There we were, probably the happiest family in the world at that moment, and I was eating up every second I could. Chris stayed by my side the entire time I was in the hospital tending to my every need. My mother came in to town to help out with the baby and for some reason I was relieved she was there. I never really depended much on my mother, but I knew she would be a great help. I ended up only being in the hospital for about three days and then they released me to go home. I never dreamed it would be that soon, but I couldn't wait to sleep in my own bed. I was so happy I wished on a star that night that nothing would ever take this happiness from me.

CHAPTER THREE

I guess the change began when Tommy was about eighteen months old. I was back to work at the shop and had a play area set up for Tommy to be with me instead of hiring a stranger to sit with him. Chris was going full speed and the company was a huge success. We had more drivers than we knew what to do with. One day a man by the name of Lucas Cunningham came to see Chris.

He was a local truck driver and had invested some money and had hit the big time. He wanted to buy a company, but wasn't too book smart and wondered if Chris wanted to expand to a new location and if they could become partners. Chris was turned off by the idea initially, but after he had time to consider all his options and had sit down with me he decided that it might actually work out. He met again with Lucas and explained that most of the startup money would have to come from him and he would have to hire his own office manager, because there was no way I would have time. They worked out all the fine print and then signed on the dotted line. They made our office simply a substation and would build a huge new office for all the drivers and office staff to have room. They included a fueling station and truck repair shop.

They hired a whole new staff and had everything up and running in no time. It was a complete success. Chris and Lucas had their offices at the new location and I decided that I would stay at the old place to keep an eye on it and also to have the freedom to come and go as I please with the baby. No one ever dreamed that this was exactly what Chris needed to hit the big time. Apparently Lucas and Chris must have shared that determination gene, because they were two peas in a pod. We decided that we needed to have a celebration and of course it would be at our house, it was the first party I had thrown since we had the baby and I was nervous about having all these people around him at the same time. I spent several days walking around the house planning, not only the best celebration ever, but also a back plan for anything that could possibly go wrong. Who knew being a mother would also make me a paranoid freak.

The day of the celebration came and went without a hitch. Everyone who was anyone was in attendance; they all had a great time and made sure to tell Chris what a wonderful party it was. I was more than willing to bow out in the shadows and let Chris soak up all the admiration, but he wouldn't hear of it. He made sure to tell everyone that his lovely wife had done it all. It seemed that having a baby not only changed me, but Chris as well. He was so much more willing to share the spotlight with me than ever before. We stood at the door and said good-bye to so many people that all the faces smeared into one big blur. I made sure to tell Chris how much I appreciated all his acknowledgment. He was an incredible man and I was lucky enough to call him mine.

One night Chris came home from work and he was covered in dirt and soaking wet. He reached over, gave me a kiss, and headed for the shower. I was only about half awake, but I knew something weird was going on and didn't know if I should ask questions or not. The next morning he came down to breakfast as if nothing ever happened. I could tell he knew what I was thinking because he shook his head and put his hand up as if to say, "Don't even ask." That made me nervous and I had a feeling that it would all come out in the open, so I put it all on the back burner for now. He headed out the door for the office and I wasn't five minutes behind him. Tommy and I spent most of the day playing and didn't really get much work done, but he is so cute he is hard to resist. Lucas called in toward the end of the day looking for Chris. I had not seen him all day and thought that he was there. He said that Chris had been there, but said he was coming over to see me. I told him maybe he stopped to bring something to eat and that I would have him call as soon as I saw him.

I sat there waiting for Chris for what seemed like an eternity when he came walking through the door nothing in hand. He told me that he drove around for a while and then came here; he needed some time to think. He looked so bewildered I wondered what he had been thinking about and I asked him. The look on his face concerned me to the point that I wasn't sure I wanted to hear what he was going to say next. He stood up and began to pace back and forth, sort of like he was going to tell me he was having an affair. That was it, I figured it out — this man is cheating on me. I grabbed Tommy from the playpen and held on to him and asked Chris what exactly was going on. He told me to sit down, because this was going to put me in shock and he didn't want me to hurt myself. I sat down in the chair and put Tommy in my lap. He must have sensed that I was becoming upset because he turned and buried his head in my chest. I reassured him that everything was all right just wishing that someone could do the same for me.

Chris looked up at me and then sat down right in front of me and grabbed my hand. He looked deep into my eyes and asked that I not say anything until he was completely done with what he had to say.

Well here it comes, I thought to myself. *He is going to tell me that he has fallen in love with someone else and that he is going to leave me. What on Earth am I going to do; I can't be a single mother and who is this chick anyway? She must be like super woman or something for him to be willing to leave ME for her.*

He began to talk, but for some reason my ears would not tune in to hear him. It was like my body was completely shutting down on me and I couldn't stop it. He was moving his hands around and then he stood up and was talking frantically and all I kept thinking was why now? Why wait until after I had Tommy are you trying to sabotage me on purpose, do you hate me that much? What kind of low life leaves a woman that is willing to do: Wait, what did he just say? I stopped my mind from racing long enough to hear him say something about drugs.

Oh my goodness what on Earth is he talking about? Suddenly my mind came out of the clouds and I could hear clear as a whistle. He was talking about meeting up with one of his old buddies who had gotten in trouble with the wrong person and he asked for Chris's help, and before he knew it he was breaking the law. He then explained the reason he had been out so late was because he was unloading all the contraband from one of our trucks that he allowed this old friend to drive from Mexico right back here to Orange County.

I could not believe my ears, was he seriously helping a convict commit yet another crime? I sat there for a minute unsure of exactly what I was going to say to him. Finally I just came right out and asked him if he was insane? What did he owe this man to risk everything we had worked so hard for? Did he realize that if he had been busted, they would both go to jail, the IRS would take our company and Tommy and I would end up on the streets? He just shook his head and told me there was no way I could ever understand, he was stuck between a rock and a hard place, there was nothing he could do, but help so this man wouldn't die.

It was as if aliens had abducted my husband, I didn't know who this man was standing in front of me. He reached in his pocket and pulled out a wad of cash. Look at all this money I made Veronica, there is more here than we know what to do with. I can't deposit it and we can't go out and spend it. I need a place to hide it for a while, because I don't know if it is clean. Holy crap now he has become a mobster right in front of my eyes. I waved my hand out at him, there was no way I wanted any part of his new illegal past time.

He said he understood and told me to go ahead and take Tommy home and he would meet up with us later. He needed to go back and make sure all of his tracks had been covered. I grabbed Tommy and we headed home. I noticed how dark and gloomy that stupid house looked from the outside. I decided I really wasn't in the mood to fix a big dinner, so we headed to the nearest diner to get something to eat. I sat at the table and watched Tommy, more playing with his food than eating, but having fun and being carefree regardless. It took a couple minutes for me to see the two men outside staring straight at me.

It took me off guard and I looked around to see if there might be someone else they were looking at, but nope, it had to be me. When I turned back to the car I could make out the face of the driver and it wasn't anyone I had ever seen before. Then I realized that it was the same car that I had seen in front of the office before. I took a long hard stare at the driver trying to let him know that I wasn't intimidated by him in the least and he seemed to acknowledge my gesture, but was not concerned by it. I felt a little anxious about leaving, especially with Tommy in tow. So I went to the manager and asked if he would mind walking me to my car. He very politely agreed and so we went. I noticed the car drive away when they saw that I wasn't alone.

When I got home Chris was already there standing in the driveway waiting on me. He ran up and opened the door and wrapped his arms around me. He said that he thought I had left him because of what he told me, and he didn't know what to do. I laughed and told him where we were and he was crazy to think he could get rid of me that easily. Once we were inside and I had Tommy settled in, I told Chris about the two men in the car outside of the restaurant and that I had seen them once before at the shop. He wasn't sure who it could be but asked that I take a picture with my phone next time I see them so he could have it traced. He of course had friends on the police force that would do anything for him. We spent that evening trying to figure out what to do with the money he had. After hours of considering all our options we decided that a safe deposit box was the best place for now. We agreed on a place to hide the key as well. It seemed that this whole mess would soon be behind us. Little did I know this was simply the beginning.

Several weeks went by without any mention of the crime and the day to day was back in full swing. Chris and Lucas were again talking about expanding the facility they were in, but instead decided it would be cheaper to expand the one I was in. We set it up so the day drivers would report to me at my shop and the long-haul drivers would still keep shop at the other office. Chris, of course, decided that he didn't like me being alone with all those creepy drivers and added an extra big office for himself. I was starting to get really tired of all the back and forth, and almost told Chris that I would prefer to just work at home. But I knew that would break his heart so I kept my thoughts to myself.

We spent so much time together on this project, it was nice and I actually started to enjoy myself. I liked the way he was with Tommy; he even bought him his own little hard hat simply because Tommy wanted it. We were a happy family again and I realized that we had made it where we wanted to be, but the boredom set in and I knew it was true for both of us.

CHAPTER FOUR

One day Lucas came into the office and said he needed to speak with Chris about something very important. I told him to go on in, so he did but shut the door behind him. I turned the radio down and listened intently to see if I could make out what they were saying.

I heard Chris say, "Absolutely not." Lucas was stating his case with great power. Whatever the conversation, they were on opposite sides of the fence about it. After about a half hour Lucas came out with a smile on his face and told me to have a nice day. I knew Lucas had won.

Chris came out and made sure that Lucas was gone and told me to make a new employee folder, but not to worry about the application because Lucas would be in charge of all that. So I made a blank employee folder and gave it to Chris, whom then left and I assumed was headed to see Lucas. When he came back later on he was not alone, he apparently had the new employee in tow. This man was huge and scared the crap out of me. Chris introduced him as Marcus Stanton, which almost made me laugh. Looking at this man and his size made me think of his name as being something like Bubba Duke not Marcus Stanton, it sounded so

21

sophisticated. Chris told me that Lucas had hired him to do a dedicated run from here to a small town in Mexico for a new company that is going to be dumping their toxic waste there.

Chris said that he would be going with him on the first haul to make sure that everything went according to plan. I agreed and said that I would be fine by myself and not to worry it was only for one night. He hugged and kissed Tommy and I, and they were off. I spent the rest of the day finishing up payroll and it was getting late, so I decided to go by some place, pick up something easy for dinner and take it home. My neighbor was outside when I got home and of course being the wife of Chris Wilson, I had to be friendly and say hello and chat for a moment. Chris' favorite saying is, "Always be friendly to everyone, you never know when you will see or need them again." He told me that the security officer was driving around because several of the neighbors had reported a dark sedan lurking around. I must have turned as white as a ghost when he said that because I knew that I had seen that car before. It was the car that had been at the office and it was also the same car that had followed us to the diner that night. I smiled and explained to my neighbor that the food was getting cold and I needed to feed Tommy. We said our goodbyes and I headed inside. I immediately went around the house and made sure all the doors and windows were locked and I set the alarm. I called Chris and told him what was going on and he said to be calm that he would call Lucas and have him come and sit at the house for a while to keep a look out for them.

I hung up with him and headed up to put Tommy to bed. I almost kept him up with me until Lucas got there, because I didn't want to be by myself. Then, motherly instincts kicked in and I knew he needed to stay on his sleep schedule. I turned on the baby monitor and headed back down stairs to clean up from dinner. I turned on the porch light for Lucas and when I did I saw the car. It was parked across the street, but as I looked closer I noticed there was no one inside. Panic began to take over and I knew that they were in my yard somewhere the question now was where? Just then I heard a commotion upstairs and I ran up to Tommy's room to make sure he was ok. Then I heard the noise again, but it was coming from the direction of our bedroom. I was frozen with fear unsure of what my next move was going to be. What would I do if there were someone in there? I didn't have any kind weapon and I was all alone with Tommy. I prayed that Lucas would hurry up and get here. I am not some kind of super woman; I am actually just the opposite I do whatever I can to avoid confrontation. I heard another noise and I knew that it was someone trying to get in. I ran down the hall toward the guest room and grabbed the cordless phone. I had the phone number for the neighborhood security guard on speed dial.

I called and told him there was someone trying to get in. He said he was on his way, but I wondered if he would get there soon enough. I needed something to use in case they got in the house before the security guard or Lucas got there. Once again I heard a noise and it sounded like a crow bar scraping up against the window.

I sneaked toward the bedroom up against the wall there was a fire place with a poker and I was going to push them right back out the window with it. I was right outside the door and my heart was beating so hard you could see it through my shirt. I was in tears trying to get up enough courage to make it through the door. I took a deep breath, leaped through door, got down on the floor and crawled over to the fireplace. I had bought heavy dark curtains after realizing my husband was a heavy sleeper. There was no way anyone could see in. I stood up, grabbed the poker, and walked over toward the window that the noise was coming from. I stood there in complete silence waiting. Waiting for someone to make their way through the window, waiting for the front door bell to ring, waiting for whatever was going to happen next. Never in my wildest dreams did I imagine that it would all happen at once. As I stood there I heard light tapping on the windowpane. I moved closer to try to make it out. I inched closer and closer and grabbed the corner of the curtain. I was going to peek out and see if I could tell what was there. As I grabbed the curtain, the doorbell rang.

It startled me and I let out a gut-wrenching scream. I bolted down the stairs toward the front door, but stopped short right in front of it.

What if it's the bad guys? If I open the door I will let them right in.

I called out — it was the security guard. I screamed through the door that the intruder was outside my bedroom window. I saw through the peep hole that he had headed over that way. I wasn't about to open the door until he caught them. I ran back toward the stairway to look out the bedroom window when the doorbell rang again. It was Lucas this time. I opened the door and told him what was going on. He headed up the stairs toward my room. I heard him yell down to the security guard there was nothing there and they must have scared them off. I knew that it was actually my scream that gave them the head start. I turned and looked out the window and noticed that the dark sedan had left as well. I sat down with Lucas and the security guard and played as if I had never seen the car before and had no idea why they were trying to get in. I really didn't know who they were or what they wanted, but I knew it wasn't a random attack. It was us they were after and we really needed to find out why.

Once we were all done and the security guard left, Lucas said that he was just going to crash in the guest room so I didn't have to be by myself. Normally I would insist that I was fine and he could leave, but after tonight I was glad he offered so I didn't have to ask. I actually slept great knowing that Lucas was right round the corner. I kept the baby monitor glued to my ear the entire night.

The next morning Lucas followed me to the office and told me to just leave the door locked until Chris got back, and to call if I saw the car again. I spent most of my time alone staring out the window, phone in hand just waiting for the car to appear. Luckily it never came. I watched as Chris and his new driver pulled up outside and was overcome with relief. I didn't want him to see exactly how upset I was so I jumped down on the floor and started playing with Tommy. He came through and swooped down and grabbed me up. He held onto me so tight just saying I'm sorry over and over again and swore he would never leave me like that again. I just sat there and soaked it all in. He always knew exactly what to say to make me feel better and that is just another reason why I loved him so much. Marcus walked in not long after that and looked like he had just seen a ghost. He told Chris that he was heading home and they could hook up later. Chris's whole persona changed in an instant and he told Marcus to call and they would meet here. That whole conversation made my stomach churn. He was such a sketchy character and I didn't trust him one bit.

Chris and I headed home where I made a huge dinner and we all sat around the dining room table and had a great meal. I couldn't help but peek out the window every couple minutes looking for the dark sedan to appear. We gave Tommy a bath, laid him in bed, and took turns reading him a story until he fell fast asleep. After that we headed into the kitchen where we cleaned together and drank some wine. I asked him about his trip and he said that everything had gone according to plan. I then asked about Marcus and what was so special that he was going through Lucas instead of the normal hiring procedures. He said that Marcus had approached Lucas and explained to him that he was a truck driver and had been for a long time before he went to jail. He said that he desperately needed a job and begged Lucas to hire him. After hearing his story Lucas couldn't turn him down. So he came to Chris and told him that he wanted to hire Marcus for this new, dedicated run we were getting. Chris was very hesitant at first, but agreed that they could put him on a trial bases for a while and see if he would pan out. I told Chris that I was not comfortable around this guy and that there something I didn't like about him. He just smirked at me and told me that after the night I had he would be surprised if ever trusted anyone new again. I knew it was much deeper than that but I didn't want to look like a paranoid freak so I left it alone. As we made our way to the living room Chris said that he had something important to discuss with me. I sat down on the couch and he sat next to me. We sat in silence for a minute and I could tell by the look on Chris's face he wanted something and it was going to cost us a lot of money. I told him to just come out with it and I wouldn't be mad regardless of what it was. He stood up and paced for a moment and then said that it would be easier to show me than tell me. So he grabbed my hand and we headed out to the car. I was clueless of what he was doing, but it was adding up pretty quickly. He hit the button to open the trunk and we walked around. As I moved closer I could see that there were several garbage bags full of something and then I realized they were full of money.

I stormed back in the house slamming the door behind. I knew where that money had come from and I wanted no part of it. I couldn't believe he had done it again only this time he had a different accomplice. "What, did you and Lucas decide that working for a living was too much so you're going to become drug dealers"? Chris said that Lucas had no idea at all what was going on and he had no plan on letting him in on the situation. He had evidently planned out every move. No matter what type of scenario I came up with Chris had the solution. He said that he didn't want for me to be too involved, but he did want me to know. He had never had secrets from me and he didn't want to start now. He said the money he would make doing this would send Tommy to any university he wanted to attend. I could go shopping any time

I wanted to. I could take any type of class I wanted to take. We could even buy a studio and I could teach classes of my own. He went on to tell me that the run would happen once a month and that he would not be driving anymore and that most of the handling would be conducted by Marcus. Chris would of course be in charge of the money and keep track of what went in and out, but other than that it was Marcus. It sounds funny, but the more he talked about it the more excited I got. I caved in after several hours of discussion and I think it was more exhaustion than actual agreeing. I told him he had to promise that no matter what happened Tommy and I could not get hurt. He said yes and if it got scary he would hire security for us. He said I didn't need to worry about a thing after all he was Chris Wilson, the man with a plan. He had calculated every obstacle that might come and knew what course of action to take regardless.

CHAPTER FIVE

We decided that we would start having a date night. No matter what was going on in our lives we would go out together on Wednesday and talk about nothing but each other. So we did every Wednesday.

The neighbor's teenage daughter would come down and sit with Tommy and we would go out for a night on the town. It was wonderful, life was simply a dream come true. Chris's new venture was going perfectly. He and Marcus were running under the radar and moving more drugs than anyone had ever seen. The drug lord that he was moving for had a special love for Chris and gave us so many lavish gifts, we finally had to tell him enough or we would have to start to explain them. Marcus of course was doing wonderfully.

The dumpsite that he would drop to said that he was always on time and had a wonderful personality. They told Chris they liked him so much that no one else was allowed to come, if Marcus was ever sick or unable to drive than Chris would be the one that would have to cover for him. Chris knew that the first couple times Marcus was stopped at the border, they would check all through the bed searching for something not supposed to be there. He also knew that there wasn't a person alive that would dig through a bag that said "Danger, toxic waste." There also wasn't a hound alive that could sniff out the drugs under the smell of all the toxins. He had thought of everything. They had a legitimate reason to drive back and forth from California to Mexico so no one really questioned their reasoning.

Our life was rapidly changing. We went from camping in the woods, to renting a motor home. We use to go fishing in our little johnboat and that changed to renting yachts to go deep-sea fishing. Our son Tommy had been accepted into one of the most prestigious preschool's in Orange County. We went house shopping in one of the wealthiest neighborhoods and fell in love with a house that was built from my imagination. It was a breath taking five bedrooms four baths, a den, and the master suite was on the ground floor. There was a finished basement and pool built for the Gods. We closed on the house and began to move in right away. We knew that leaving our old neighborhood would be hard, but it was a step in the right direction for us.

Once we got settled in we decided to begin our old routine. Taking walks in the evenings stopping and visiting with all the neighbors. This was definitely a world away from where we came from. It was more a competition of who has more, than a conversation. Chris was right where he belonged, he knew that he could talk smack to anyone, anytime, anywhere. I of course felt out of my league. All of these women had charities they were president of and they were president of their children's PTA, not to mention all the campaigning they did for their husbands. I just stood there shaking my head in disbelief. I mean I knew these type of women existed, but I never dreamed I would end up living next door to them. I nodded and explained that I really needed to get Tommy home. Chris caught my drift and said good-bye to all his new playmates and agreed that they would meet again real soon. They never had a chance, instantly taken in by Chris's charm.

I still had my doubts about Marcus and I kept up my guard, but decided that we could be friends. He would be in the office with me and Tommy would spend every minute chasing him and playing with him. Tommy adored Marcus and he didn't seem to mind the company. Tommy and Marcus were best friends and it was kind of nice to have him cling to someone besides me for a change. Chris wasn't as accepting of this new friendship as I was. He would always call for Tommy when he would start chasing after Marcus. I honestly think that Chris was a little jealous. I don't think Chris had ever had to deal with being second choice and didn't how to handle it. I kind of enjoyed it myself because it made my husband look almost human. We had our routine down to the point that it wasn't even thought of as a crime, (to us any way). Marcus and Chris were in charge of one business and Lucas was the partner in the other. It was uncanny how Chris could keep record of both in his head and knew how to keep them both running successfully and without a hitch. God must have had a plan for this man because of how incredibly smart as he was. I was still a little nervous about getting caught and Chris would reassure me that there was absolutely nothing to worry about. I smiled but always had the idea tucked away in the back of my brain.

One day as I driving home from the office I noticed a police car following behind me. I had Tommy in the car in a car seat and we were both buckled up. I was doing the speed limit so I knew there wasn't any noticeable reason for him to pull me over. When his lights came on I panicked. I knew that we had been busted and that I was going to jail for a long time. I merged to the side of the road and put the car in park. I reached into the glove box and got all of my paper work ready. As I sat up I noticed the officer staring at the license plate. Why was he staring at the plate, I thought, he must be memorizing it so if I take off he can catch me. I was not the type of lady that would do well in prison I mean I would be the girlfriend in no time. He finally came to the window and motioned for me to roll it down. "Miss, do you know why I pulled you over"? The officer asked. Well yes because I'm hardened criminal and you are going to read me my rights and take me to jail, I thought to myself. "No sir I don't", I said to him. "Well your license plate expired last month, were you aware of this"? He had such a smug grin on his face when he asked me this I just wanted to smack him. "It must have totally slipped my mind officer, but I promise it will be the first thing I take care of in the morning." I flashed my most innocent smile and he let me go with a warning, but told me that I would get a ticket next time. I pulled away and started laughing and just couldn't quit. I think it was relief that I wasn't going to jail taking over. When Chris got home I told him all about what happened and he also started laughing at me. He said I could have some time off from work to take care of my family life, but not to make a habit of it. I just shoved him and gave him an evil stare.

It was Wednesday and I was really excited. Chris said he was taking me somewhere I had never been before. He said after tonight we would start a whole new relationship and it would be so much stronger than I had ever known before. I was so curious I couldn't pay attention to much of anything all day. I kept asking little questions to try and figure out what he was up to. I asked what I should wear and he said whatever makes you comfortable, so I knew it wasn't something fancy. I asked him how I should fix my hair and he just smiled. I sat there at my desk for a while trying to think of where we could be going that wasn't fancy and I had never been before. It was too much to bare I couldn't wait I am not good with surprises. I wanted to know where we were going and I wanted to know then. I leaned back in my chair and looked in Chris's office. He was on the phone with someone and it looked like a pretty serious conversation. That really sucked because I wanted to ask some more questions before we left. I never got the chance to ask anything because by the time he got off the phone it was time to leave. We went to the house got changed and ready to go. The neighbor came down to babysit and we were off. I walked over toward the car and Chris laughed at me. He said that we were walking to our date tonight. I laughed at him and opened the car door and sat down inside. Chris looked at me and smiled and took off walking down the road.

I yelled for him and he turned around and held out his hand out for me. I couldn't believe this man was actually going to make me walk. I had on high heels and they weren't the comfortable walk around kind either. He told me we had a couple minutes if I wanted to change into something more comfortable and warm, because we were going to be outside most of the night. I was in shock where on Earth was he taking me? I went in the house and put on a sweater, some jeans, and my walking shoes. He said that I would be much better off in this outfit, but he didn't want to offend me earlier. I probably would have killed him if I had to walk around in those heels all night so he was lucky.

As we made our way down the street I noticed that there were several other neighbors headed in the same direction. Ok Chris now can you please tell me where we are going, I asked. He told me to be patient and I would see in a moment. Sure enough as we rounded the corner there were several people standing in the road. It had been blocked off and there was music playing and drinks stands set up everywhere. People were coming in packs bringing food and gifts. It was some kind of party I figured that one out, but who were the presents for and why hadn't we brought one. Chris turned and looked at me and said surprise. It's a block party to welcome us to the neighborhood I told you it would be worth it. It was the nicest thing I had ever seen before. Here was a party for my husband and I, but the best part was I didn't have to do any of the planning or set up. The real test would be if I had to help clean up. All the neighbors came and introduced themselves and told us where they lived. We got to meet some really influential people here in Orange County, which Chris loved. The party was beautiful and the gifts were wonderful.

We danced, and drank, and socialized. It was almost better than one of my parties (almost). We stayed until pretty much everyone else had gone home. My husband was having the time of his life and me as well. We said our good nights to the host and were off. We lay in bed that night and Chris looked at me and told me there would never be a woman that could hold a candle to the love he had for me. As always he knew exactly what I needed to hear, and I slept like a baby that night.

CHAPTER SIX

The next day was a little shady to start with and I had a strange feeling that it was only going to get worse. Chris left a little earlier than I did and so I decided that a couple of extra minutes getting ready wouldn't hurt. I took my time eating breakfast and taking a shower and getting Tommy ready as well.

We finally got to the office about an hour later than we normally did and Chris was not pleased. He told me not to get used to it because he needed me here on time every day. That was actually the first time he had spoken to me as an employee and not his wife. It actually kind of turned me on. I put Tommy in the playpen and he went back to sleep. So I made my way over to the boss and told him that I would do whatever it took to keep this job. I knew that Chris loved role-playing and of course he took it hook, line, and sinker. We made our way into his office, but not before the doorbell began to ring.

I looked at the monitor to see who it was; it was an older distinguished looking gentleman. When he turned his face to the screen though, you could tell that his years had not been good to him. I asked through the intercom for his name, when he gave it all the blood from my body froze. It was Tony Patino the most recognized drug dealer this side of the Grand Canyon. He looked a lot different than what I had pictured. When I pictured this man I saw evil eyes and horrible scars all over his face. He spoke with a gangster like slang and had the look of death throughout his whole being. This man standing in front of the office was nothing like that.

He was a rather attractive man and spoke like he could be an attorney or something. Finally Chris tapped me and told me to open the door. I looked at him and with great hesitation; I hit the button to unlock the door. Mr. Patino entered with such presence; I almost couldn't catch my breath. He walked in and stood directly in front of me then he looked down at me and smiled. I cringed at the thought of what this man could do to me and asked him what I could do for him. He snickered a bit and said that it was my husband he was looking for and asked to speak with him. I phoned into Chris's office and told him that Mr. Patino was requesting a meeting with him. Chris was calm and told me to escort him in. Well there was no way I was going to do that, I pointed to the door and told him to go right on in. He nodded a thank you to me and went in.

I sat in my chair frozen for what seemed like an eternity. I held my breath trying very hard to hear what they were saying. Chris of course had shut the door and when his door is shut I couldn't really hear what was going on, (I hated it when he did that). Tony hadn't made any type of gesture to me as to why he would be here. I obviously had a huge inkling as to the reason for his surprise visit, but didn't want to bring myself to think it out loud. Tommy started to stir and I knew once he was awake it was the end of ease dropping for me. I reached in and pulled Tommy out and set him in my lap. I grabbed some of his toys from the diaper bag and got down on the floor with him to play. My stomach started to churn in knots, I felt completely out in the open with him and knew that if something went wrong and bullets started to fly Tommy and I were right in the line of fire. I wished that someone important would call so I could interrupt this crazy meeting and send Mr. Patino on his way. I actually thought about calling Lucas and telling him what was going on so he could interrupt, but I knew that would lead to more questions that I really didn't want to answer. I heard Chris raise his voice in a way that I had never heard before. He was yelling at the top of his lungs and it scared me. I gathered all of Tommy's things and headed out the door. I was going home and I would call and check on Chris later.

As I walked out the door toward my car, I saw it. There was the car, the same one that was at the diner and also parked outside my house the night someone tried to break in. I almost passed out right there; I couldn't believe this man was coming here in that car like I wouldn't notice it. I turned around and went back inside. I stood in the doorway for a moment trying to decide what my next move was going to be. Before I could even make up my mind; Tony came storming out of the office, and stopped right in front of me. He told me that my husband was making a huge mistake, smiled, and then walked toward the car. I took Tommy and walked inside to set him down in the playpen with his toys and walked into Chris's office. He was sitting behind his desk with his head in his hands.

I wasn't sure if I should say anything but I was so frightened that I had to. I told him about the car in the parking lot and how it was the same car that had been following me around. I told him that it was the same car that was parked in front of our house the night of the robbery and that this Mr. Patino was up to no good and I didn't ever want to see him around again. Chris came from behind the desk and wrapped his arms around me. He said Tony had made a business proposition with him, but Chris knew Tony was not trustworthy and he turned down his offer. He said Tony told him he would be sorry, but there wasn't anything that man could do to hurt us right and not to worry. Unfortunately his words of encouragement just weren't enough this time. I knew that Tony wanted in on what we were doing and he wanted it bad. A man like that will not simply give up when it comes to money.

Chris and I finished up at the shop and he said the he needed to go by and see Lucas for a while and told me to just head on home. So Tommy and I loaded up in the car and I took a quick look around to see if the stalker car was there. The parking lot was clear other than mine. I headed out and tried to decide what sounded good to eat. I went through a fast food drive thru and headed home. I looked up toward the sky and noticed how absolutely still everything seemed. The leaves on the trees weren't blowing and you couldn't hear a single animal. It made me shiver inside, of all the nights for Chris to come late he picked tonight. I pulled into to the neighborhood and saw the security guard sitting in the booth at the front. I waved to him as I went by and almost felt as if I would never see him again. My stomach was in knots now trying to shake this feeling I had forming all over me. I pulled into the driveway and took a quick look around for the car and it was not there.

I walked inside and headed toward the kitchen table and stopped dead in my tracks. There sitting at my dining room table was a man. He was enormous in size with straight jet-black hair that was even longer than mine, His arms were as big a round as my waist, and he must have been at least 7 foot tall or more. I had no clue who this man was or why he was in my house, but I didn't plan on sticking around to find out. I dropped the food and headed for the front door with Tommy in my arms. I reached the threshold of the door and there was another man standing there waiting for me. He looked to be a lot smaller than the other one and smelled like he hadn't seen a shower in years. My heart fell to the floor and my eyes shot around looking for a way to get out, but the two men had me trapped. I turned to the bigger man and asked him why he was here. He said that his employer had asked them to pay me a visit. I knew to whom he was referring and what this visit was in reference to and I was infuriated. How dare that man think he could send these two bozos to my house and then allow them to just break in and walk around like they owned the place? I told him that my husband would be home any minute and then they would wish they had never met us. The skinny one just laughed and grabbed my arm. I tried to free myself, but he tightened his grip. He then led me into the kitchen and told me to have a seat. The two men sat in front of me and the big one began to speak. He told me that his employer had a sit down with my husband earlier that day and that he was not pleased with the outcome of the meeting and so these two were sent to persuade me to change my husband's mind. I couldn't believe what I was hearing. I looked down at Tommy and he had no clue what was going on. He was looking at the skinny one like he wanted to play. I turned him around to face me, but it didn't take him long to turn the other way. Were these thugs honestly trying to get me to convince my husband to go into business with Tony the creep?

Quickly I turned to the skinny one told him that I thought working with Tony was a good idea and I had no problem talking to my husband and as a matter of fact he would be home soon and they could talk to him then. He shook his head in disbelief and I knew it wasn't going to be that easy. I yearned for Chris to come walking through the door right then and get rid of these freaky guys because they were really starting to scare me. I felt my phone in my pocket and told the guys I needed to use the rest room. The big guy told me to leave Tommy with him and the skinny guy would go with me because with all the windows in the house there was no way I was going by myself. I told him I would hold it because there was no way I was peeing in front of a stranger. He told me to have a seat; we needed to finish our little chat. I knew that this was not going to end well and I needed some way to get them out without either Tommy or I getting hurt. The two men continued to tell me how this deal was going to work. They explained how easy it was to get to us and if they had to come back for a visit again there would be blood. They said that Mr. Patino was a reasonable man and all he wanted was a small cut of the profit. He knew we were making quite a bit off this run and he wanted his take for keeping quiet. I told them that it wasn't a big deal and we had no problem sharing and I would have Chris draw up an agreement in the morning. They both stood up and said that Mr. Patino would be back to visit Chris in the morning and they hoped that they would never have to visit under these circumstances again. I simply nodded and prayed that they would be leaving. They said goodnight and walked right out the front door. I fell to the floors in tears. I was so distraught I didn't even hear my phone ringing. It was my mother calling to chat, I told her that I had a horrible headache and I would talk with her tomorrow. I hung up with her and turned around to call Chris. I instantly got his voicemail and knew that he was still at the shop with Lucas and there was no telling how long he was going to be there.

I collected myself and picked our dinner up off the floor, by now it was freezing cold. I threw it in the trash and looked for something to heat up quickly. Tommy and I ate and I took him up and put him to sleep. I was in the kitchen cleaning up from dinner when Chris came home. He came in the door and I walked up to him and smacked him in the face. I was so upset he had broken a promise to me and was nowhere around when I needed him most. His reaction was understandable he was of course completely stunned, he had no clue what had went on and I had full intention of telling him, I just wanted him to see what I was greeted with. He wanted to know exactly what he had done to deserve that and so I started telling him everything. All about the way that they were in our home and how I was alone with Tommy and no type of protection. How I felt completely invaded and didn't even want to sleep here tonight. How I had tried to call him and got sent to voicemail. How could he start a venture like he had and have no clue that someone would be displeased and want to hurt us? He left me alone and vulnerable not knowing if I was going to die or even worse, if they were going to hurt Tommy. He reached over and put his arms around me and told me how sorry he was and that he was going to take care of everything.

He went and checked the house and found out how those men got in and said that from now on, we could not leave this house without setting the alarm. They had cut what they thought was the cord to it, but that was just a dummy. Chris had the guy that installed the system put the wire in underground so it couldn't be cut and if the alarm had been set they would have set it off and would have gone to jail. He then picked up the phone and called Marcus and told him to come over right away. We all sat in the living room and Chris asked Marcus exactly what kind of character this Tony guy was. Marcus said when he got out of jail, Tony's thugs approached him with an offer to run some drugs for him and make some big money. He was on the streets with nothing so the offer was exactly what he needed at the time. Well Marcus was well known in the neighborhood and he earned "street cred" quickly.

He was making quite a profit and Tony wasn't happy with it. He told Marcus that if he didn't start paying him back for all the money he had stolen that Marcus would pay. Unconcerned by Tony's threats Marcus continued to make money off the drugs he was selling for Tony and even had his own place finally. He met him a nice girl and they decided to settle down together and Marcus wanted to get a legitimate job and marry her. That was right around the time he ran in to Chris again. They had been high school friends and Marcus was trying to find a way to pay Tony back and get out of the game for good. He did the run and paid Tony every last dime. Tony told him there was no way he could get out now because he knew too much and when Marcus refused him, Tony sent his thugs in to kill his girlfriend. Marcus was heartbroken and tried to go after Tony. But he was too protected so he left him alone. He moved out of the house he and his girlfriend had and into a dumpy little apartment. He had come back to talk Chris again, but ran into Lucas instead. He really needed to straighten out his life and knew that Chris would be the one to help him.

"Ok wait a minute, hold the phone; I didn't realize that you were the one that did the first run. I thought that was someone else. So then all of this is your fault! You are the one that brought all this drug and mobster crap around my husband." I was furious at this point, I knew there was something I hadn't liked about this guy and now I knew what it was. He was scum, a bottom feeder, looking to make a buck off my husband. He wasn't Chris's friend, he was a horrible person and he needed to find someone else to give him a hand out, I am sure he had made enough money off of us to be comfortable for a while. I walked out on the conversation because I had heard all that I needed to. After Mr. Bottom feeder left I was going to tell Chris that this was the end we were not going to get into this any deeper or someone was bound to get hurt.

Finally, after the boys talked out all their planning, Marcus headed home. I sat down on the couch next to Chris and told him I was done. "This whole thing is getting scary Chris, and I don't want something horrible to happen that we can't take back." He agreed with me, but told me it wasn't going to be easy to give up. He told me that this run was going too smoothly for his investor to simply let us walk away from it so we needed to come up with a plan. Somehow we had to convince this man that it was getting too risky and that someone had found out about us and we needed to lay low. Once we had that arranged we needed to cover our tracks and completely clear ourselves of anything to do with the run. "Does that mean all the money we've saved as well?" I asked him. He said not to worry about the money that he had a way of taking care of it and no one would be able to trace it. I was so scared I told him that Tony was going to be paying him a visit tomorrow and that if he didn't start sharing with him; I was going to end up like Marcus's girlfriend. He just shook his head and told me not to worry. There was no way those men would ever get that close to me again.

CHAPTER SEVEN

The next morning I woke up not feeling so well, I knew what was wrong, but I couldn't get rid of the feeling. Chris told me to take a pill and suck it up because there was no way he was leaving me home alone. So I went in the bathroom took some aspirin and headed in to get Tommy ready. We left the house and headed toward work, I noticed the gas was getting low and I told Chris to stop and get some but he was running late so he said we'd stop on the way home.

As we pulled into the parking lot of the office, Mr. Patino and his thugs were already there waiting for us. It was that same car and when we drove past I noticed that the driver was the skinny guy from the house and he was the same man that had been following me before. I told Chris I was afraid and really didn't want to be here. He said not to worry, that as long as we were together he wouldn't go after me. We pulled into our spot, unloaded and headed inside. Mr. Patino followed right behind us. He grabbed the door from my hand and yanked it. I turned to him and gave him a nasty look, this man was on my last nerve and I had taken all that I was going to take from him, mobster or not. He walked pasted me and laughed as he headed toward Chris's office right behind him. Tony turned to close the door and Chris told him not to because he wanted to keep an eye on me.

"Some pretty nasty people tried to intimidate my wife last night and I want to make sure they don't try something that stupid again", he said.

Tony must have been upset by what he said because he started right at Chris making idle threats and explaining how bad he could damage us if we didn't comply with him.

My husband told him simply "Look Mr. Patino I know you think that by going into my home and threatening my wife we were going to give into to you, but unfortunately for you my decision has not changed. I feel you are a liar and a cheat and I will never in my life have any type of association with you especially any type of business venture. So if you would kindly take yourself and all of your employees away from my property, I will try to refrain from calling the police."

Wow, I had never been more proud of my husband than I was at that very moment. He stood so proud and strong and I almost wanted to yell "in your face" to that nasty man, but I just sat there with the biggest grin on my face instead. Apparently Tony was not impressed with his boldness and bid him a warning before he stomped out the door.

"As I told your lovely wife last night, I didn't want to have to pay her a visit again, but you have left me no choice. I promise you there will come a moment that she will be vulnerable and that will be the moment that we strike. I am a reasonable man but you have pushed me to no return and I will make your life a living hell from now on."

He turned away from Chris and headed out toward me almost like he was going to hit me. I saw an opportunity and I wasn't going to let it pass me by. I stood up and told him that I was not afraid of him or the idiots that worked for him and if he wanted to come after me than he could bring it. Oh the smile that came over his face was terrifying, you could see the ice coming from his soul and I knew that I was in trouble. He slammed the door as he left and made Tommy cry. I then started to cry myself and Chris came over and picked up the baby and handed me a tissue. He told me not to worry he was going to be interviewing for security today and he would make sure to get nothing short of the best.

I spent the rest of the day staring at my computer screen and imagining all the scary things that this man could do to me. As the applicants came through one at a time, they were all interested in the position until Chris explained whom they were going to be protecting me from and then all of a sudden they didn't want it anymore. It was so bad that when one of the men heard Tony's name, he took off running out the door. I was so upset and ready to call it quits when the last applicant came in. He was tall, built and very handsome. I gave him a big smile and told him to have a seat and Mr. Wilson would be with him shortly. Chris heard me and peeked around the corner.

He wasn't a jealous kind of man, but it was fun to push his buttons every now and then. He said that his name was Daniel Davis and he was former military. He had just moved here from Florida and was looking for a job when he heard about us. Chris came out of his office and started asking Mr. Davis several questions about his training and background and all of that. This man was Special Forces and was well trained in combat. Chris was impressed with him and I really liked him as well. Chris said that he only had one more question and if he answered it correctly than the job was his. He asked Daniel if he knew who Tony Patino was. Daniel looked at him with a confused look and told him he had never heard of this man and asked if he was the reason that we needed a bodyguard. Chris smiled with relief and replied, "Yes he has threatened my wife and my son so I want to make sure they are protected at all times." Daniel told him that he would do whatever it took to keep that man away from me and so Chris hired him right there on the spot.

Daniel left and said that he could start first thing in the morning, which wasn't a problem since the day was pretty much over. Chris and I finished up some last minute details and decided to call it a day. I packed up Tommy's things and loaded them in the car while Chris locked up the shop and we were off. We were going to stop at a little Italian restaurant that we both loved, but it was quite a bit away so we stopped at the gas station to fill up the tank. Chris got out to pump the gas and I told him I would go in and pay because I needed to use the rest room while we were there. He agreed and said he would keep an eye on Tommy so I didn't have to take him in with me. I heard the chime of the front door to the convenient store and it echoed in my ear. I felt a chill come over me and I stood there for a moment and was about to turn back to the car, but knew I really need to go. I walked up to the register and handed the man some money to pay for the gas and asked where the rest rooms were. He handed me this stick that had a key on the bottom of it and said that they were around back. In these moments I wished I were a man; they can use the bathroom anywhere. I turned the corner and put the key in the door. As I turned the knob I felt a hand come around my shoulder and then everything went dark.

As I came to I realized that I was in the trunk of a car. I felt around with my hands trying to see if I could find anything to free myself with. I felt toward the back seat and felt a tire iron. It was one with four ends on it and I pulled it toward me. The trunk was so dark and sweltering I felt like I could hardly breathe. I felt the panic starting to set in and paranoia took over. I didn't know whose car I was in or where they were taking me. All I knew was I needed to get out of there fast. I lifted the crow bar above my head and toward the lock of the trunk. I tried to finagle the lock open, but it wouldn't budge. So I started slamming the bar at it trying to make it pop open and that wouldn't work either. Then the car came to a stop and I got really still. I wondered if they had heard me beating at the trunk and were coming to make me be quite. I heard the engine shut off and some one step out of the car. I listened to see if they were walking my way but they weren't. I could hear the footsteps walking the opposite direction of me.

Once I couldn't hear them anymore I started to bang the crowbar on the lock again. I knew that this was getting me nowhere fast and I needed to come up with a better plan. I felt around again for something, anything that might give me an idea. I felt toward the top of the trunk and I could feel some wires and so I moved the fabric back and pulled on the wires until they came loose. I tried to push up on the roof of the trunk thinking that the wires released it, but that was not the case. Again I heard the footsteps, but they were coming toward me this time. I laid there focused on the sound coming closer and closer. I was so afraid I couldn't even swallow. I heard them stop right out in front of me and then I heard a set of keys jingle. The lock came undone and up came the hood, outside stood a very dark figure. He reached in and told me to stand up; he grabbed a hold of my arm and pulled me out. He pulled my arms behind me and slapped some handcuffs on me. Then he pushed me forward, but didn't say a word. I could see a house in front of me and it was real creepy looking.

The stairway that led to the front door was hanging on it last limb and the shutters were all but gone. We walked in through the front door and there was nothing to decorate the room except for a chair and tiny television. He sat me down in the chair and handcuffed me to it and said to just sit tight for moment. I had never seen this man before, but I was confident as to why I was there. Mr. Patino came inside and walked over to me. He stood there for a moment and then hauled off and punched me right in the jaw. The pain from the blow was excruciating and I thought for sure he had broken my jaw. I looked up and asked him why he had done that. He just shook his head and told me that I already knew exactly why I was here and why he had hit me. He was through playing games with amateurs and was going to get what he wanted one way or another. The man that brought me here walked out of the room and I was left alone with Tony. I searched the room for some sort of escape route and came up short. The only way out was the same way I came in and Tony was blocking that. I needed a plan, but what was I going to do? I was handcuffed to a chair and there was a mad man standing in front of me and I was certain that he was going to kill me.

The other man came back in to the room but he wasn't alone. He had brought Marcus in with him. What was he going to do with Marcus? Was he going to kill him, the same way he had his girlfriend? I didn't like what I had gotten into and if I made it out of here alive I was going to kill Chris for involving me in this stupidity. I told him when he started this stupid thing that someone was going to get hurt. Little did I know at the time that it would wind up being me. I wasn't ready to die; my son hadn't even started school yet. He needed me and there was no way I was going to let these idiots take me away from him. Just then a thought came to me when I saw the gun on the waistband of the new guy.

I looked at Tony and told him that I'd never had the opportunity to use the restroom and could I please go now. He nodded to the new guy and told him that he and Marcus would be in the other room when we were finished. This was it my only chance to get away and I had to act fast. He lifted me up and put the cuffs around my hands and led me toward the hallway. As I got to the threshold of the bathroom, I explained to the man that I couldn't go with my hands behind my back. So he did just what I wanted him to do. He turned me around to face away from him and started to unlock the cuffs. As I freed one of my hands I grabbed him and quickly turned around. I pulled his gun loose and shot him right in the head. The gun must have already had a silencer because it hardly made a sound. I took the other handcuff off and headed down the hallway to the room that Tony and Marcus were in. I stood up against the wall and listened to what they were saying. Tony was asking Marcus how he could have made such a stupid mistake in picking us. He knew that Chris wasn't going to take my kidnapping lying down and it was going to be war. Marcus said that he didn't remember Chris being so savvy and that he had changed quite a bit from the man he used to know. I couldn't believe my ears, Marcus was working with Tony but what were they up to? I saw the back door and I headed out and ran up the road to a neighbor's house and called Chris.

Not even five minutes later the police were surrounding the house that Tony was in and Chris was right behind them. He ran up and grabbed me so tight and it looked like he had tears in his eyes. We headed toward the police officer coming out of the house and he said that there was no one inside. Obviously when they discovered I was missing, they took off.

I gave the police my statement and they told me that I would not be brought up on charges for killing that man because it was a case of self-defense. Chris asked the police if they were going to pursue this and they said yes, but they needed a name and description of all the men involved. I hadn't really thought about the fact that Marcus had been working with Tony until now and I knew that if I told the police about him that he would tell them about our little after hour's operation. So I told them that it had only been Tony and the other thug.

They said that they knew exactly who Tony was and they had been after him for years and that they were glad they finally had something to charge him on. Chris told the police he was taking me home and that we would be there if they had any more questions. So he led me to the car and we headed home. The babysitter was at the house with Tommy and I ran in and picked him and held on for dear life. I had never been so happy to see him because for a while I thought I would never have the opportunity again.

Chris and I sat down in the living room and he started to tell me how it all was his fault and how guilty he felt for letting it happen. He told me that Daniel was going to be with me 24 hours a day whether Chris was with me or not. He vowed that Tony was going to pay for what he did and he was going to hit him where it hurt. Daniel emerged from the kitchen and told Chris that he was ready. Chris reached over and kissed me and said he would be back shortly and to not ask any questions. He then told Daniel not to let me out of his sight for even a second. Daniel nodded and Chris was gone.

I lay down next to Tommy on the floor and we watched one of his favorite Disney movies together and I fell asleep. Later on when I woke up I didn't feel Tommy next to me and I jolted up. I saw Tommy on the couch playing next to Daniel and they were having a good time. He said that Tommy had woken up a little before me and knew I was tired so he decided to keep him entertained until I was awake. That was so sweet for this man who barely knew me to already have such care for my family. We sat there for a long time talking about family and his time in the military and I actually began to feel a little safe again. I knew in my heart that this man would be willing to do whatever it took to keep us safe and it was such a nice feeling to have after what I had been through.

I told Daniel that I really needed to take a shower and asked if he minded being with Tommy for a minute. He said that wasn't a problem but he had one condition. He wanted to sit in my bedroom with the baby while I was in shower so he could keep an ear on both of us. It seemed a little awkward, but not unreasonable and I agreed. We headed up the stairs toward my room and he stopped me. He entered into the bedroom and then went into the bathroom.

He checked behind the door and looked out through the window and then gave me the all clear. He asked how to turn the television on to give me a little bit of privacy. So I turned it on a cartoon and went to the bathroom. I ran a really hot bath and settle in to the water. My head fell hard against the pillow and my body felt like pure filth. I lay there soaking in the bubbles and relaxed. I heard a strange noise and my senses became heightened when I heard it again. It was almost like a muffled cry or something so I sat up to get a better signal. Then I heard a man scream and the sound of a gunshot. I jumped out of the water threw my robe around me and ran out to save my baby.

As I walked in the bedroom Daniel stood up and ran in the bathroom behind me. I saw the show he was watching and knew that was where the screams had come from. Daniel came out of the bathroom and asked me what was going on. I started laughing uncontrollably and then broke down in tears. I told him what I had heard and the thought that was in my mind and he too laughed. "I am so sorry, how selfish of me, I never even took a second to think that this movie might scare you; please don't be mad I promise it will never happen again." I wiped me face and told him not to fret I was just jumpy and paranoid. I headed back in the bathroom and took a quick shower. It was getting pretty late, so I told Daniel I needed to get started on dinner. We went in the kitchen and Daniel sat at the table while I put Tommy in the playpen. I of course headed to the refrigerator and pulled out the necessary ingredients for a fabulous dinner. We talked some more about this and that, it was nice having someone there to talk with while I was cooking. I turned when I saw the car pull into the drive way and Daniel told me to relax it was just Chris. Now how crazy is it that this man could recognize my husband's car faster than I could.

Chris came barreling through the door completely out of breath and talking a million miles a minute. Daniel told him to sit down and relax. Daniel asked him if he had taken care of everything and

Chris shook his head yes. He asked me if I was doing ok and I smiled and said yes. Chris wanted to go upstairs and clean up before dinner and headed out. Daniel stayed down stairs with Tommy and me and helped set the table. The three of us were all seated and waiting for Chris. He came down the stairs and looked a lot more collected than he did when he first came through the door. I asked him what on Earth was going on and if I needed to be prepared for the police to come knocking on the door soon. He said I had nothing to worry about and not to ask any questions and definitely not to talk to anyone for a while. We had to maintain a low profile for the time being and everything would work out to our advantage in the long run. I wasn't sure what he had done and at this point I didn't want to know. The way I saw it was if the police asked me any questions I could pass a lie detector test when I said I knew nothing. We sat together and had a wonderful meal; I looked at my husband and son and thanked God that I was given another chance to be with them.

I took Tommy upstairs to get him ready for bed while Daniel and Chris headed into the office for a meeting. I put Tommy in the bath and we sang and played and had a good time. With all the excitement and commotion of the day he was so tired that when I tried to put his clothes on all I could manage were the pants. So I put him down in his bed and he was out like a light. I sat down next to him and just watched him as he slept thinking of all the things I would have missed out on had I not returned home — all the years of school and little league, his first girlfriend and his first broken heart. How he would be brilliant and fly through school with honors and be accepted all the top colleges — watching him graduate and then venture out on his own into this great big world. Then the day when he would come to me and tell me that he found the one. He would introduce her to me and of course I would think she wasn't good enough for him, but would love her anyways and then they would be married. I wiped the tears from my eyes and reached over to kiss him good night. My baby was such a precious gift and I would never lose sight of that.

I wandered around the house picking up all the little odds and ends that were out of place like all of Tommy toys and Chris's clothes. Then I headed in to clear the table from dinner and I felt Chris's eyes on me. I turned around and sure enough there he was watching me the way he did when I worked in the tavern. We shared a smile and he came over to me and rubbed his hand across my face. His swelled up with tears and he actually started to cry. He swore that he would never lose me again and couldn't even fathom what life would have been like without me. He had such a soft caress as he held me and I just fell into his arms. I knew that nothing could ever feel as safe as his arms and that was where I always wanted to stay. He told me not to worry about the mess and he would help me in the morning. So we headed off to bed. Daniel had set up camp in the guest room which was right between ours and Tommy's room. He had also turned on the baby monitor in Tommy's room, but Chris said he was not putting one in ours. "You really don't want to be able to hear in our room", Chris said to him.

The next morning I woke up and Chris was already down stairs. So I got up and headed into Tommy's room, but he wasn't there. So I headed down stairs to see what everyone was up to. Chris was in the kitchen making breakfast and singing like a fool while Tommy danced around him. Daniel was at the table with his face buried in the newspaper and trying not to laugh. The dining room was immaculate and even the dishes had been washed and put away. I asked Chris who he was and what he had done with my husband and what time he planned on going to work. He walked over sat me down at the table and said that we were taking the day off. As long as we had had this company we hadn't had a whole day together and it was high time we did. From now on, once a month, we were going to a family day; one that would not include the office, but would include the three of us, having fun. Well I was all for that, but what had brought this on. As if on cue Daniel got up and walked out to the back porch and shut the door behind him taking the newspaper and his cup of coffee. My husband sat down at the table next to me and grabbed my hand. "The day you disappeared was the worst day of my life; I had no idea where you were or if I was ever going to see you again. So I made a promise to God that if he allowed me to be with you again I would not take advantage of you and would treat you like the precious gift you are. Veronica you are the rock and foundation of this family and without you it would all fall apart. I knew the moment I saw you that you were a powerful force but I never told you how much meant to me. So from now on I am going to be the husband I am supposed to be for you." It must have been too much for him because he got up and went over to the stove and started packing pancakes on a plate. I reached down and picked up Tommy and sat him in his chair and we all had a great breakfast.

We took a picnic down to the lake and were feeding the ducks when Chris's phone rang. It was Lucas and I told Chris to answer it because it might be important. Lucas said that there were a couple of federal agents at the shop and they wanted to speak with Chris right away. So we loaded up and headed home. Chris dropped all of us at the house and headed into work. A couple hours passed and Chris came pulling in the drive way. He came in the house and told us to have a seat because we really needed to talk. He said the feds had received an anonymous tip that we were running drugs from Mexico in our trucks and that they had a warrant to search all the vehicles and records that we had at the shop. He also said that they were going to question everyone at the shop and that included me. He said that he bought me a couple of days by explaining the ordeal I had just been through. I remembered Marcus and what he had said at the house that day. I told Chris about it, but for some reason he didn't seem the least surprised. "Did you hear what I said to you just now? Marcus, your driver is working for Tony. He was in on kidnapping me and he has been working with Tony even before he came to work with us." I couldn't understand why Chris wasn't at the least upset that the man he trusted to run this operation was in business with the man that tried to kill me. "Listen Veronica there is going to be a lot that you will find out in the next few days. What I need for you to do most of all is to trust me. I promised you from the beginning that I would never do anything to hurt you or Tommy and I meant that."

The next couple of days went by in a haze. There were people in and out of the office taking everything and tearing up whatever they got their hands on. I told Chris that it was too much for me and I would be at home until all this mess was done. As I headed to the door though one of the officers stopped me and asked if my name was Veronica Wilson? I said yes and he told me that I would need to go down town with him for some questioning. Chris said there was no way I was going anywhere. The officer pulled out a document and told Chris that I was going either willing or in cuffs. So I told him not to worry I would go and answer their questions and then head home. He said that wouldn't be a problem as long as Daniel could go. They agreed and we were off.

It was actually kind of exciting; I had never been in a police car before. Daniel and I had to ride in the back behind the cage. I started messing with people on the ride there. When we would pass someone I would mouth the word help to them and the reactions I got were priceless. Daniel caught on to what I was doing and he started doing it too. I guess the officer didn't find it amusing when he figured out what we were doing and asked us nicely to stop. Once we got to the station it was so picturesque, everything looked just like it did on television. There was a huge desk in the front that held an information sign above it. Then as you passed all the little desks with police officer sitting typing intently on their computers, you saw a row of four rooms with doors. He stopped in front of the very first one and held the door open for us. Daniel and I went in and sat down at the table in the center of the room. That was all they had in there along with a hanging light right above it.

Holy crap, I felt like I was in an episode of law and order or something. Sure enough a detective came in the room holding a file folder and he had it opened going through the contents. He sat down across the table from us and continued reading for a moment and I just couldn't control my urge, I broke out in laughter and that caught his attention. He asked me what I found so amusing. I apologized and told him about the whole law and order thing and well he didn't find it as funny as I did so I restrained myself from making a joke out of anything from then on. He started asking question like how long I had been married and how long we had owned the company. He then started asking a bunch of questions about Marcus, like how I knew him and why we had decided to hire a convict. I answered the questions just like Chris and I had rehearsed and the entire interview went without a hitch. He offered to give us a ride home and we accepted. Since the first police man wasn't impressed by our little game on the ride there I figured this one wouldn't be either, so I just did some site seeing out the window.

When we pulled in the driveway Chris was already there. He greeted us at the door and asked me if I was ok. I told him the whole story about the ride there and back and also about the law and order thing and he laughed so it must not have been that bad. I told him all the questions they had asked and my answers and he just smiled. He said I was a trooper and then told me he had a couple of really important errands to run, but he would be right back. Daniel walked him out to the car and then came back in.

The next day at the office we spent most of the morning cleaning up the mess the police had left behind. They said they had all they needed and would be in contact with us soon. They had taken all the computers and all the payroll reports for the last three years. They also took any accounting records we had and all the employee files. I was so afraid that they would figure out what was going on and we all end up in jail forever. I know Chris had told me to trust that he had everything under control, but that was easier said than done. One of the drivers came in and gave us his resignation stating that he couldn't continue working for someone who associates with criminals and he left.

Not long after that the phone rang; it was Lucas telling Chris that the police had Marcus in custody. They talked for a minute and then he hung up. He told me that it would all be over soon. He told Daniel to be on the lookout for anything fishy and he needed to leave to take care of business.

Daniel and I sat in the office for a while and Lucas came driving up. He got out of the car and ran inside. Chris came pulling right behind him. They said that had a friend at the police station who said that Marcus gave up Tony on everything. He told them all about my kidnapping and about Tony killing his girlfriend. He told them all about Tony's business like who he sold to and who his connections were. He agreed to go into protective custody, but wanted to make a stop first. Chris wasn't exactly certain, but thought that he was going to come here. Lucas said he needed to make a run to the other office and would be back soon. Daniel reached in his coat pocket and handed Chris a gun. "This is for just in case", Daniel told him. Chris asked Daniel to take us home, but a car pulled into the parking lot before we could leave. So Daniel, Tommy, and I headed back into Chris's office and locked the door. I heard the door open and then I heard Marcus's voice. You could hear the anger in Chris's voice as he spoke to Marcus asking him how he could have done it. "I gave you everything you could ever ask for and you betrayed me. She is my wife and you hurt her." I had never heard Chris so angry before and I was so afraid. Marcus was pleading with him asking for forgiveness and telling him that it really wasn't his fault it was all Tony's idea, he didn't know about it until he saw me at the house. I heard a punch and then someone hit the floor. I ran to the door, but Daniel pushed me back. I wasn't sure what was going happen, if Marcus was going to hurt Chris or what. They argued back and forth for a long time and then silence. We sat right inside the door for a moment and then Marcus spoke.

"Honestly you asshole I was getting really tired of sitting by and watching you have it all. Why was it fair that you got all the money and success, while I sat by and took the crumbs you gave me, I was the one taking all the risks? Then to make it even worse, you got to have Veronica, too.

What about me what about my girlfriend. You didn't do anything when you heard that Tony had killed her, so why should I put my neck on the line for your girl?" The shot rang out so loudly it almost seemed unreal at first. Everything stood still for a moment and then started to play out in slow motion. Daniel reached down and pulled me back away from the door and dove on top of Tommy and I. He told us to get under the desk. Then he stood up and took a gun out from his boot and headed out into the main office. "Oh my God Chris what happened." I thought for sure that Marcus had shot my husband and now he was lying there dying.

I grabbed Tommy up and headed into the office expecting to find my husband bleeding on the ground. My heart was beating so loudly I couldn't hear anything but the thumps. Daniel came over and tried to stop me, but I pushed past him. Then I saw Chris crouched down on one knee over Marcus. Marcus was the one who had been shot. That meant that if Chris wasn't the one who had been shot, then he must have been the one who did the shooting. The front door burst open and several police officers came through and grabbed my husband. I tried to stop them, but they just pushed me back. They handcuffed him and walked him out the door. Some

E.M.T's came through and collected Marcus's body, he was dead. I was in complete shock how on Earth could this have happened. My husband wasn't a murderer he was a good man. This must be a dream and I wanted to wake up.

This wasn't a dream though it was reality and I was right in the middle of it. Lucas came in and asked what happened. I told him that Chris had killed Marcus and as the words came out of my mouth the tears came out of my eyes. Lucas told me that he was going to drive us home and then he was going to call an attorney and meet up with him at the police station. He told me not to worry; he would take care of everything. This time I didn't believe a word of it. Chris had been telling me for years not to worry and then he goes and murders someone. It was a disaster and I had idea how to make it right.

CHAPTER EIGHT

Chris's attorney had him plead not guilty, by reason of temporary insanity. The anger he had built up from my kidnapping came out when Marcus confronted him. The judge ordered him to spend 10 years in a hospital, but he could get out in as little as 3-5 years for good behavior.

I went to see Chris a few days later to let him know that the case against us was dismissed due to lack of evidence. He smiled at me and told me he was sorry.

"I am truly sorry Veronica; this really was not part of plan at all. When Marcus told me that he had no concern for your safety I saw red and the gun in my hand went off. I didn't want to kill him, but I wanted him to pay for what he had done to you."

Chris was a man with a plan always. He calculated every step he took in life and I knew that going off plan was something new for him and I didn't know how this would affect him. I also couldn't help but be mad at him for leaving me alone, how could I keep the company running by myself? How were Tommy and I going to survive with no type of income?" He said that I needed to go and talk to Lucas, that they had made arrangements that would take care of everything while he was away. He laughed and told me that I had to promise that I wouldn't fall in love with anyone else while he was away. He knew my heart belonged to him and there was no way I could ever love anyone but him. Tommy reached up hugged Chris and I saw his eye swell up again. "Do me a favor Veronica, I will only ask you for one thing while I'm gone, but it is a big one." I told him I would do anything he asked me to. "Make sure my son remembers who I am and please don't ever let him know what I did. I don't want him thinking that I am that kind of man." I made him that promise and then we left. I headed to the office to meet with Lucas because he said that we had some things to discuss.

I walked in the door and the blood stain was still on the floor. Lucas said that he was having the carpet replaced in the morning, but everything else had been cleaned and taken care of. I asked him what he needed to see me about and he told me to have a seat. He told me that Chris had made up a power of attorney for me that stated if he was ever unable to take care of his self that I would become the main signer on everything. So I was now owner of this shop and co-owner of the other. Lucas had no problem helping in any way that I needed. He said that Daniel had agreed to stay on as our bodyguard until Tony was caught.

He said that I was smart enough to figure out the rest for myself. I had a thought come to mind, Chris had told me before that we couldn't just walk away from the drug game and I didn't want to have two drug dealers coming after me. I decided that it was beneficial to let Lucas in on what we had been doing and maybe he could help figure out a way to get away from it. So I told Lucas everything about the run. He listened to me and held on to every word until I was through. "Wow Veronica sounds to me like you have gotten yourself into quite a pickle." What, is that really all he has to say to that? Surely he must think I'm joking or something I mean if I were him I would be furious right now. He shook his head and started laughing, and that made me mad. I wasn't telling him a funny story this was real and I was scared. I mean I knew Tony would try to come after me knowing Chris was in jail and I couldn't do this run with Marcus out of the picture and so this other dealer was going to come after me too. On top of that I didn't even know who this man was that I needed to look out for. Lucas put his hand on my shoulder and said "Don't you worry Veronica I may be a drug dealer, but I am in no way a killer. If you want to be done with this than by all means I can do it alone."

"But, we can keep it going if you want to."

CHAPTER NINE

We sat in the corridor for what seemed like an eternity waiting to see Chris. It was only me and Tommy there waiting, the pain and hurt stabbed my stomach harder and harder with every second that passed. Tommy was growing aggravated and I didn't know how much longer he could wait. I had gotten there a lot earlier than expected. Lucas had been to visit Chris the day before to have him sign all the final paperwork and go over every last detail before the transfer could legally take place. He said that Chris was in good spirits and looked well for his condition.

What condition is that? He isn't sick, he is in prison. He killed someone and now he is facing hard time and I am left out here on my own to try and take over everything that he has built.

The doors finally opened and we were all told to sit at separate tables and wait for our loved ones to come through the opposing doors. It was like sitting at the circus waiting for them to release the animals. Tommy sat down in my lap and buried his face in my chest. I didn't know if he was fully aware of why we were there. He was still so young and naïve. Looking closely through the doors I could see the inmates lining up one by one to come in and see their families. I looked around the room and noticed the people sitting at the other tables. At the table across from me sat an older woman and a younger looking man. They were on different benches looking in different directions not saying a word. Just in front of them was a middle-aged couple sitting together, the husband had his wife's right hand clasped in his and he was caressing it and talking very gently to her. All the tables were occupied. Some looked happy while others were sad; I could feel the anticipation in the room growing.

When the inmates were let in, I was so happy to finally get to put my arms around my husband, but also worried that he wouldn't be the same man. Chris was toward the back of line and I was beginning to wonder if he had come. Then I could see his face, it was so handsome even now. I lifted Tommy's head and told him to look up. He saw Chris and was out of my lap running toward his father. Chris knelt down and scooped Tommy up and they just stood there for a moment. Tommy clutched his father's neck tighter than I had ever seen before. Chris started to make his way over to me with Tommy still attached. I stood up and wrapped my arms around him. His smell was so familiar and comforting. I didn't want to leave that moment, but he released from the embrace and sat down in front of me. I sat back down and reached across for his hand. He held on and we sat there just looking at each other.

He broke the silence by asking if I had seen Lucas since yesterday. I told him I hadn't yet, but was supposed to meet with him later on that afternoon. He simply shook his head and then changed the conversation. We talked for a long time and Tommy kept interrupting, telling his dad all about everything he could think of. Chris would look at him and listen with his full and undivided attention and Tommy just ate it up. It was such a wonderful visit, but it didn't last long enough.

The guard called the five-minute warning and Chris's demeanor turned serious. He told me to make sure that I kept the meeting with Lucas. He said to make sure that I had Daniel with me at all times no matter what. He put great emphasis on the last part. I asked him what was going on, but he told me not to worry that Lucas was taking care of it. The guard stood up and walked over to the door. Just like trained lions, the inmates began to rise up and say their goodbyes. Chris wasn't one to make a scene so he simply handed Tommy over to me then he kissed us both. We embraced for a warm hug and he told me to go.

"I love and miss you both all the time," he said, and then turned to walk away.

The guard opened the door and one by one the inmates disappeared. As I was leaving I turned back to see if I could catch a glimpse of Chris one more time, but he was already gone.

I held onto Tommy and walked out into the parking lot and froze. I looked around rapidly trying to find where it was coming from. I felt there was someone watching me and waiting. It was horrible. Daniel had been standing up against the car, but was right in front of me now asking what was going on. I was so frozen with fear, I couldn't even speak. All I could do was turn my head around and try to find them. Daniel snapped his fingers in my face and it brought me out of my trance.

"What's going on?" Daniel asked.

"I just feel like someone's watching me, waiting," I hesitated, but told him my fear.

"Get in," he said as he forcefully grabbed onto Tommy's hand and mine. He flung us both into the car and was out of there like a bat out of hell. Once he felt we were safe he pulled over and called Lucas. He stood outside the car with a gun in one hand and his phone in the other. I knew something was going on and I was about to find out exactly what it was.

We drove away in complete silence. I had so many emotions flowing through me all at once that it almost made me sick. I looked over at Tommy, who had absolutely no idea what was going on. He was off in his own little world, playing with his toys, and showing me what all they could do. Daniel kept glancing at us through the mirror. I final got up the nerve to ask.

"Why did you freak out back there?" I asked, leaning toward the mirror so he could see my face. "Is there something going on that you aren't telling me about? You need to be up front right now," I quietly demanded.

He continued driving as if he hadn't heard a word I said.

I scooted back in my seat and continued to watch Tommy play with his toys.

When we arrived at the house, Lucas was waiting there to walk in with us.

He sat down in the living room and asked both of us to join him.

"Tony has been spotted around town by different people," Lucas spoke quietly. "I've put you and Daniel on high alert — especially since Chris is away."

"Why hasn't anyone said anything to me about this until now?" I was furious. "Especially my so-called partner who was supposed to be on my side," I shot a sarcastic look at both of them and then went on a tirade yelling and screaming.

"You two are here to help me, not control me," I yelled and then stormed off.

We ate dinner in silence, everyone trying their best to avoid any kind of eye contact. Tommy, of course, thought it was some sort of game and began screaming and laughing when someone would look at him. It was so cute that we all kind of gave up on being mad and started playing with him. We sat around in the living room and came to the conclusion that from now on I would be included in all conversations as long as I promised to do what I was told which was meant to keep me and Tommy out of danger. Daniel and I said goodnight to Lucas and I headed off to my room. Shortly, Daniel appeared in the doorway to apologize.

"All is forgiven," I said. "Don't worry so much."

He nodded and headed off to his room.

CHAPTER 10

The next morning was my first day back to work as the owner since Chris was arrested. I woke up dreading the day but headed down stairs for coffee. Like a sonic bomb the emptiness of the house hit me. I remembered back to the mornings I would come down and see Chris at the table, coffee in one hand and the morning paper in the other. I would sneak up behind and kiss him on the head. He would reach up and rub my arm, not moving his eyes from the paper at all.

I looked around the room for even a small glimpse of him, but nothing was there. It was almost as if he had never been there at all. I grabbed my coffee and went back upstairs for a quick shower before Tommy woke up. Our morning routine was quite the norm and we were out the door.

Lucas was already waiting in the parking lot when we arrived at the office.

"Why didn't you just go in?" I asked.

"Waiting on the new driver," Lucas spoke, "to go over the directions for his run."

My heart automatically sank deep down in my stomach. I could tell by the look on his face which run he was referring to. I rolled my eyes and headed in. I had not been back to the office since that day Chris was arrested and taken away. Someone had done an excellent job of cleaning up. I walked around surveying the room for a moment thinking about that horrible day when my world came crashing down around me. The memories started flooding back and it was almost as if there was a projection screen in front of me playing it back. I could see Chris standing in the center of the room telling Daniel to get Tommy and me out. I could see the three of us running into Chris's office to hide.

As the memory played, I realized I was holding my breath almost as if I was waiting to hear the gunshot ring out again. My trance was interrupted when Tommy cried out for me. I tried to just laugh off the horrible feeling and then headed to my desk. Lucas came in and sat down in front of me. You could tell he had something serious on his mind.

"I have a new driver coming in to take over the run from here to Mexico," Lucas said, then smiled and just sort of let that statement sit in the air and simmer for a minute.

He said he had made arrangements with his supplier in Mexico to start the process over again, but things would work a lot differently this time. The driver would be made to believe that there was hazardous waste going both ways from two different companies. He said he needed to know if I was still willing to help him out with this or not. I thought for sure after the all the police investigating he wouldn't ever think of doing this again, but he did. He had thought so much about this that he had covered all the details and really didn't need me for much at all. I knew that if Chris were here he would be more than willing to do anything for Lucas and so I felt sort of obligated to him. I agreed but only if he'd guarantee that we couldn't get caught. Both of Tommy's parents didn't need to be sitting in jail.

He agreed and also promised that if anything happened only he would be held responsible. We went through all the pros and cons of what could happen and it was nice. It felt like the way Chris and I used to discuss things. I must have wandered off into my own little world because soon Lucas was calling my name and waving his hand in front of my face. I laughed at him and started back into our conversation. Tommy was down on the floor looking up at Lucas intensely and so he reached over and picked him up. They sat in the chair together for a moment just looking at each other in a way I had never seen before. It was almost like Tommy couldn't remember how he knew him for some reason. Then he reached up, gave Lucas a big hug and then wanted down again. Lucas looked at me for an answer but that whole situation was new to me. It was as if he'd discovered something brand new.

Lucas asked me to go into Chris's office and grab the folder for the Mexico run. I just sat there frozen for a moment not realizing that I hadn't even passed my office all today. I looked at the door to Chris's old office and started to cry. Lucas rubbed my shoulder and he stood up to go and retrieve the file himself, but I stopped him. I knew I would eventually have to go in there. It was probably best there was someone present when I did. I collected my feelings and stood up, trying my hardest to look confident and strong, all the while knowing that the first sight of anything that reminded me of Chris would cause me to crack. I walked closer to the door and grabbed the handle. As the door creaked open my heart began to race faster.

My legs were like noodles holding me up. I pushed it opened all the way and took a quick look around. Everything was exactly how Chris left it. The bookshelf in the corner held all his books and photographs. On the second shelf in the corner was Tommy's first drawing framed with pride. His desk was perfect, the phone in its place, the computer right in the center, and of course our wedding photo to the right where everyone could see it. He knew exactly how he wanted his office set up and he spared no feelings making sure it was done correctly. I sat down in his chair and there was still a hint of his smell lingering there. I opened his file drawer and located the one Lucas wanted. As I closed the drawer I noticed that the middle one was slightly ajar. I peeked in to see what was caught and pulled out a photograph. It was one he had taken the night he first asked me out. I smiled so brightly and turned it over to read the caption.

"The love of my life forever and always, she will be mine"

He had kept this picture the entire time. I was so taken back at the fact that he had indeed been in love with me the whole time. We had been together for so long and I never realized how deeply he felt for me.

I came out of his office with a smile and the folder. Lucas cocked his head sideways at me and then he smiled back. I thought for a moment, but I knew it was him that had pulled that picture out purposely for me to find it.

"Thank you," I said, then handed him the file.

He nodded and headed out the door.

Daniel was at the other desk working steadily on something so I decided to leave him alone for the time being. We finished out the day and went home. Not feeling well, I asked Daniel if he minded keeping an eye on Tommy for a bit so I could rest in a bath.

"Not at all," he answered. The two of them then went into the living room for some play time. I headed up the stairs. I ran the hottest water I could stand and sank slowly in until all of my body was fully immersed. I soaked in the water going over the events of the day trying to decipher what exactly I had agreed to. Was I actually going to go back to the life of crime, wondering everyday if this was the day I would be arrested and hauled off to jail?

Lucas had promised he would be held accountable, but what if they discovered that I had a hand in all of it. What would become of Tommy and me then? I heard a bell in the background, but I shrugged it off to my mind paying tricks on me — until I heard Daniel at my bedroom door, knocking and telling me there was someone at the front he didn't recognize. I quickly hopped out and wrapped my robe around me. As I headed down the stairs Daniel was right behind me with Tommy in one hand and his gun in the other. I reached the front door and peeked out through the peep hole.

She rang the doorbell again only this time she gave attitude with it. I almost shrieked at the sight of her. Daniel stood there aiming to fire and I motioned for him to put the gun away so I could open the door.

"I know you're home," she bellowed through the door. "You need to come and open this door immediately."

I took a deep breath and opened the door. There standing right in front of me was my mother and father. She slammed the door wide open and pulled me in for a hug, then pulled back to size me up real quick. She looked at me and what I was wearing and then turned to looked at Daniel. She insisted on knowing who he was and why exactly he was with Chris's wife in a robe. Daniel's face turned bright red and he was absolutely speechless. Finally, my father interrupted and reached around my mother to hug me.

"How have you been?" he asked. "How's Tommy?"

Tommy had his head buried deep in Daniel's shoulder which did nothing to persuade my mother that nothing was going on. She reached in to grab him and Tommy screamed out at the top of his lungs, clinging even more tightly to Daniel. I introduced Daniel to my parents and invited them in so I could shut the door.

"Let me go get dressed," I said, heading up the stairs.

I knew I couldn't leave Daniel with my mother for very long or there would be Hell to pay. I almost broke my toe changing but I was done in a flash and rushed back down the stairs. As I turned the corner to the living room I could hear my mother and father laughing hysterically at whatever Daniel was saying. I stood behind the wall for a minute, listening and smiling under my breath. It had only taken him about five minutes to win them over — I was impressed. My father told Daniel that he was sure he must be a good man if Chris felt comfortable enough to leave him here with me while he was away. That one simply made me rolls my eyes. Ever since the day Chris and my father met, they were instant family. Almost as if Chris were their natural son and I was the daughter-in-law. I joined my parents in the living room and we were all deciding on where to dine for the evening when the doorbell rang again. I threw Daniel a quick look so he would not pull out his gun again, then I walked to the door. Lucas was out front trying to look back at me in the little peephole. I laughed and opened the door to ask him in, but he pushed past me. He came in ranting about how amazing this new driver was and how well he believed everything was going to work. He was cut off when he noticed we were not alone in the house. My father was on his feet already headed in to see who exactly this idiot was. My mother was sitting in her favorite position eyes fixated on this scum that was standing in her son's house like he owned the place.

Lucas introduced himself to my parents, who were not as willing to accept him as had been Daniel. Realizing my parents' reaction, I explained that Lucas was in fact Chris's business partner which in turn meant he was my business partner for the time being. My father understood and shook his hand. My mother wanted to know why he was here after hours at night with my husband not being home. Mom was always very old fashioned, believing that women should simply fall behind their men and no other should interfere in their personal life. She continued her evil stare at him, but Lucas was not at all afraid of this woman. If she knew what type of person he really was she would be a little less combative.

My father invited him to join us for dinner and he accepted. We drove in two separate cars. My mother and I rode with Daniel and

Tommy, while my father and Lucas took his car. We met in front of the restaurant and walked in together. We actually had a wonderful time despite the snares sent between my mom and Lucas. Afterwards we all headed home minus Lucas, who said he would see me tomorrow. I asked my parents how long they planned on staying and if they wanted be at the house or not. My mom insisted they would stay at the house with me until my husband came home. My heart sank. I don't think she truly understood that it was going to be a long time before Chris came back, but I just let it go and showed them to the guest room then went on to bed.

The following morning I woke up the same way and headed to the kitchen for coffee. Only this time instead of being empty and lonely, my mother was there waiting for me with breakfast and piping hot coffee. I had to admit it was nice having her there. She was my mother after all, the woman who took care of me for so many years. If Chris couldn't be there to take care of me then she was the obvious choice to take over. I sat down as she filled my plate and set it in front of me.

Then she placed my coffee in front of me and kissed the top of my head. It was so comforting and warm to feel her next to me. I ate my pancakes and asked for seconds just like I did when I was a little girl. I could have gotten lost in my childhood for the rest of the day with her, but I knew I had to go to work. She sat next to me with a very curious look and asked if she could keep Tommy for the day so he could get to know his grandparents. It was kind of a surprise to me, because Tommy had spent every waking moment of his life with me so far and I hadn't even realized it.

She was pleading to me with her eyes and I just had to give in. She jumped up with joy and I laughed as I headed up the stairs to get ready. She was right on my heels but stopped at Tommy's room. There was no telling what she had planned but I knew he would have a blast and probably be spoiled rotten by the end of the day.

Daniel and I headed out and met Lucas at the shop. The new driver was starting and, of course, Lucas would be making the first run with him to make sure it all went off without a hitch. After all the arrangements were made Lucas and the new driver were off. I told myself I was not going to get too personal with this one — that way I wouldn't get hurt. I spent most of the day playing catch up on billing and payroll. I knew I could get all this done before Lucas came back and then we could get started on all the rest. I told Daniel I wanted to go out to eat at lunch so we went to one of his favorites – a bunch of cheap tacos and a salad bar. I made a mental note to never ask Daniel where he wanted to go again.

The day flew by and before I knew it, it was time to go home. I checked the lock on the door, set the alarm and turned toward the car. I noticed Daniel running toward me with his gun aimed away. My first instinct was to duck, and so I did. Good thing I listened because the shot barely missed my head. My ears were screaming from the passing bullet and I was disoriented to the point that I fell. Daniel grabbed me and put me in the car and we took off. He was driving and shooting at the same time. I was in the floor with my head completely covered.

He was driving like a maniac trying to lose these freaks, but nothing worked. As we drove through the gate at the front of our subdivision the guard watched as we raced by. He tried to yell for Daniel's attention, but there was no stopping him. The guard saw the other car coming behind us and he called the police, and then got in his car to chase them. We pulled in the driveway sideways and Daniel jumped out and told me to head inside. I looked up and saw my mother with Tommy in her arms standing in the doorway trying to walk toward us. I knew the other car was only seconds behind so I stood and screamed at my mother to get back in the house and ran as fast as I could behind her. I dove in the doorway just before the shots began again and shut the door. My father motioned for us to go upstairs and we did. I grabbed Tommy from my mom and we ran into my room and locked the door. Sitting there in the silence, waiting was horrifying. I had no idea what was going on outside. It brought back such awful memories of the night Chris left. We weren't in there for long when my father knocked on the door and announced himself. My mother stood and opened the door for him. The first moment, he could, my father embraced my mother and they held on tight.

I knew my parents loved each other, but it was nice to see it every once in a while. He reached down and helped me up and said the police wanted a word with me. So I handed Tommy off to my father and went back down stairs. As I made my way out the front door it looked like a standoff was going on. There were at least ten police cars out front.

My car looked like a slice of Swiss and I gasped as I looked at all the holes where I had just been sitting minutes before. A detective introduced himself and asked what my recollection of the day was. I told him every last detail I could remember, but I had not really seen much buried down in the floor of the car. He thanked me, handed me his card and told me to call if I remembered anything else. I surveyed the damage and didn't see Daniel at all.

I walked around the scene wondering what could have happened to him. I motioned for the officer to come back and asked him where my driver had been taken, but I saw him out of the corner of my eye before I finished the sentence. He apparently had been grazed by one of the bullets and had been seen by one of the emergency officers. I was relieved that nothing worse had happened and we headed back inside with everyone else. The police were there for a little while longer until finally everything was cleared. I knew the neighbors were hysterical, trying to figure out what was going on. I knew I would be hearing from the association soon enough. The day had been too much to take and I went to bed directly after I lay Tommy down.

I woke up with my head whirling through the events from the day before while trying to plan my day ahead. Coffee was weak. I made a different, pot a lot stronger. My shower was invigorating, but not as helpful as I would have hoped. My mother, of course, asked to keep Tommy again and said that he would be better off at home with her for now until things settled down a bit. I knew she was right. Our house was built like Fort Knox and my parents would give their lives for Tommy. Daniel and I went on our way to the office.

Every car we passed I watch like a hawk just waiting for the bullets to start flying. The police never caught the people who were shooting at us, but we knew they were some of Tony's men. Lucas was looking into it. He was, of course, there waiting for me to find out what happened and if we were all okay. It had been a nightmare and the last thing I wanted to do was rehash all the ugly details so I just waved him away.

The day was mostly a blur —people's faces coming in and out of focus. I honestly should have just spent the day at home with my family, but I knew with the new driver coming in tonight by himself for the first time, Lucas would want me at the office. I heard the horn coming down the road and I knew he was back. I stood up to head out with Lucas, but Daniel stopped me and *he* went out instead. For a moment I got pretty upset, thinking that Daniel was trying to take over, but then I knew he was only trying to protect me. I sat in my chair waiting for them to finish what they needed to do and it left me with nothing to do but think. It seemed that the fun Chris and I had when we were doing this as a couple had disappeared the night he was arrested. Being a part of this run now made me feel like I was betraying him. I told myself right then that I was changing my mind I didn't want to do it anymore.

CHAPTER 11

We left the shop and headed home almost in slow motion. I looked to the clouds and they looked to be following us waiting to spray us with rain and shoot us with lightning. The winds howled loudly and pushed the car back and forth. It seemed there was an unseen force trying to keep us from getting home. I told Daniel I had a horrible feeling in my gut. I couldn't put my finger on what it was exactly but I was uneasy and in a hurry to get home.

He nodded and sped up a bit. The security guard at the front entrance tilted his hat to us as we drove by and had a peculiar smile. My heart was racing and my hands were sweating profusely. I almost got out and started to run but I knew the house was right around the corner. As we rounded the last bend I could see there were absolutely no lights on and the front door was standing wide open. Daniel stopped the car dead.

He jumped out and told me to get down and cover myself until he came back. I did as he said, but wasn't sure if I would be able to wait for him. I got down on the floor as far as I could and covered my head. Daniel reached in and locked the doors and was gone. I sat there completely covered trying to swallow my stomach back down to where it was supposed to be. Time seemed to last for an eternity but I finally heard Daniel's footsteps coming back. He knocked on the door and hollered out that it was clear for me to come out. I made my way out of the car and turned to head toward the house when I noticed my mother standing in the front yard but there was no Tommy. I assumed he was still napping, but as I got closer to her I could see tears in her eyes. She refused to meet my gaze and I looked around to find my father but he was nowhere in sight.

Daniel was walking right behind as if he was waiting for me to fall and that is when it hit me. I took off like lightning, past my mom, through the front door, and straight up the stairs. I rushed into Tommy's room and pulled up the covers, but he wasn't there. I ran into my parents room no Tommy, I rushed across into my room and he wasn't there either. I started screaming his name all around the house with no prevail. Daniel was waiting for me at the bottom of the stairs holding a piece of paper. I slowly walked toward him panicking more with each step. I stopped and stood completely motionless hoping that if I didn't move then the reality couldn't come true. He met me half way and took me down the rest and we went into the living room. He sat me down on the coach and handed me the paper. Without saying a word I opened it to read what it had to say. It read just like I knew it would. Someone had taken my son and now they were demanding money. Once I had completely finished the contents I knew that it wasn't just someone, but the same man who had kidnapped me not long ago and was still on the run. Now this man had taken my son and wanted to set a meeting for us so he could tell me in person exactly what he wanted.

I had never needed my husband more than this moment right now. My mother was standing in the doorway waiting for me to respond, but all I could do is reach for her. She came in and sat down next to me and threw her arms around me, apologizing for letting them take him. I knew it wasn't her fault I knew if she would have been capable she would have stopped them; my father too. But where was he? I hadn't seen him since I got home. I asked my mother where he was and if he was alright. She shook her head and tears came rolling again. He had put up quite a fight and they had beaten him terribly but otherwise not hurt.

She said that he was in the study too upset to face me. I knew the only person in this world who could make me feel safe right now was him. So I stood up and headed out after him. I swung the study door open wide and found him erect facing the fire place. I rushed over and wrapped my arms around him and the tears came flowing like a river. He to cried and we stood there together wrapped tightly, not knowing what to do next. I told him he was not to blame and we were going to get the son-of-a-bitch who took my son one way or another. Daniel came in and said that the meeting time was fast approaching and we needed to leave. The note stipulated that we meet in public so no one could get any ideas about contacting the police. He agreed for Daniel to come, but that was it. We were to meet right at 5p.m. no later, no earlier. He would make his demands and my son would be returned when they were met. My father insisted that he come along but I assured him we would be fine — Daniel wouldn't let anyone hurt me.

As we got in the car Daniel turned to me with a look I had never seen before from him — fear. He handed a gun to me and told me to put it in my purse. I pushed it away but he pushed back saying it was only for an emergency. I took it and put it in my purse. He said that if somehow Tony was to get his hands on me as well, then it would all be over. Tony would hold all the cards and we would all be in serious trouble. He didn't know what Tony's plan of action was and he wanted to make sure that we were both prepared for anything. We arrived at the restaurant and I felt this sort of stinging in my gut as I got out of the car and we headed through the front door. It was a small restaurant and there weren't a lot of people there, but enough to bear witness to any wrong doing. I set eyes on Tony as soon as we were in and headed right over to him. I'm not exactly sure what came over me, but I instantly reached over and smacked him right across the face. He laughed and told me to have a seat before I caused a scene. Daniel looked to be in total shock but had a hint of pride, too. Tony proceeded to tell me that Tommy was safe and unharmed but would not remain that way for long unless I agreed to meet with every demand. I told him to lay out his cards and we would talk. He said he was entitled to part of the money we had collected doing the run to Mexico, seeing as it was his idea in the first place. He wanted his share up front. He knew we were at it again and he wanted in for as long as we were.

"Money is nothing – just a material thing," I said. "If you want it then I'll give it to you …"

Daniel stopped me mid-sentence.

"I want proof that Tommy is okay," Daniel demanded. "You won't see a dime until we get him back."

Daniel and Tony had a stare off and finally Tony spoke. He motioned for one of the waters to come over to the table. He mockingly told the waiter that we ordered some proof and to make it a rush. The man pulled out his cellular phone and opened it. There on this tiny little screen was my Tommy. He was so afraid and his face was swollen from the tears. He had a cloth over his eyes and tape over his mouth.

"Let me talk to him," I was furious. "I can calm him down."

The man then unmuted the phone and moved in closer to make sure that Tommy would hear my voice.

"Don't worry, Mommy will be there soon," I said to my son through the phone.

The man slammed the phone in my face and walked away. Tony stood up and came closer to me. I could feel his horrid breath on my face. Daniel stood up to grab him, but Tony's men stopped him.

"You have 48 hours to get the money to me, or else," he said and then walked away.

"We need to leave," Daniel scowled at the wall for a minute and then spoke.

***

My dad was pacing back and forth in front of the window when we arrived home. My mother was right inside the doorway and was out in the driveway even before we got out of the car. She looked so disappointed when I didn't have Tommy with me. My father immediately started with the third-degree questioning, wanting to know exactly what happened and what our plan of action was going to be. Daniel walked into the kitchen kind of oddly, so I lurked behind the wall peeking in to see what he was up to. He was in a very serious conversation with someone on the phone. He was going over the situation and then agreed to meet this person, once all of us had fallen asleep. I knew in my gut who he was talking to and felt that I should have been included in the conversation.

As soon as he hung up the phone, I walked around the corner. He knew what I was thinking and sort of smirked at me.

"I just got off the phone with Lucas and he is well aware of the situation," Daniel said. "He has it under control."

"Absolutely not!" I yelled. "Tommy is my son and if anything is going to be handled, I will be the one to handle it."

I knew if Chris were here he would automatically take charge and know exactly what to do. I was the only thing Tommy had right now and I was not about to sit idly by and let the men take care of it, especially since he wasn't their child. Daniel insisted that I didn't need to try and be brave, but bravery didn't have anything to do with it. I was going after Tony full force to make sure he paid this time.

"He got away with kidnapping me but there's no way on Earth I'm going to let him get away this time," I insisted.

Daniel finally understood and agreed to let me go along to the meeting.

***

It was going on midnight when we got together. Lucas was, of course, surprised to see me. He and Daniel exchanged a quick look, and then sat down. We decided the office was the best place for us to meet. We were comfortable there and if, for some reason, Tony had someone following us, they would assume we were trying to get the money. The office felt a lot colder and wetter to me. I had actually never been there after hours. We sat around for a long time trying to decide on what our best move would be. Lucas said he had contacts on the police force that he could get in touch with through back channels. That way, they'd be involved, but not noticed. Daniel knew people from his days in the service that lived for this sort of thing. They were talking about going after Tony instead of paying him.

"We will give the money to Tony so I can get Tommy back," I demanded as I stood between the two of them. "I don't care what you do after that."

They had nothing personally to lose. I didn't think they could be reasonable about how to approach the situation. I made sure they were clear on my feelings.

"We are not to tell Chris about any of this under any circumstances," Lucas ordered.

"No way," I argued. "If my husband found out something like this happened and I wasn't up front with him about it, he would never trust me again."

I would want to know and I had no intention of hiding it from him.

I agreed to set up the drop before I spoke with him, but I was going to see him as soon as we got Tommy back.

***

After hours of going back and forth on what was going to happen, we all came to an agreement we could live with. I would pay the ransom to Tony and get Tommy back. Then Daniel and Lucas could do whatever they felt needed to be done. I didn't really want to be at work the next day, but Lucas demanded that we carry on with life as usual to keep from raising any suspensions. My parents said that they could no longer bear to watch what all was happening and would be going home once we got Tommy was home and safe.

At the office it was the same old routine — drivers coming in for assignments and checks. Our new driver for the Mexico route was good. He was always on time and clueless as to what was going on — we liked it that way. So did our contact in Mexico. Lucas had it set up so perfectly that the driver even had invoices to sign. I would never admit it, but he had this run set up so much better than Chris ever could have. I had spoken with Tony earlier in the day and had the meeting set up for later that evening. He agreed that we would exchange the money for Tommy, "easy and quick."

I would have Daniel with me and he would have one of his men with him as well. I was so anxious to see my son again; I couldn't concentrate on anything else. I was pleasant to the drivers and even sparked conversation with some of them to try and make the day go by a little faster. Unfortunately, it didn't help and the hours dragged on — it was excruciating.

A half hour before drop off and my stomach was twisted all in knots. My heart was pounding out of my chest and I was pacing back and forth, watching each minute go by one by one. Daniel told me to get ready so we could head out. I grabbed the bag full of money and my purse. Daniel asked if I still had the gun; I nodded. I had never fired a gun before but I honestly believed that if something went wrong tonight I was going to pull it out and let loose on all those people.

The car set out for our destination and I sat right next to Daniel on this drive instead of riding in the back. I wanted to make sure I didn't miss a thing. I wanted to see everyone who was there and everything that happened. I wanted to feel in control. I wanted to feel if something went wrong, I would know the exact second it happened.

We rolled into the garage parking lot and headed to the very top where we were told to meet. We inched our way up the floors through the parking lot each one a little closer than the other. Neither one of us spoke a single word for the entire trip. We both stared intently out the windshield looking for something or anything that wasn't supposed to be there. Each car was a threat, especially if it was moving. I held my purse in my lap and gripped the gun tightly. For some reason, it just made me feel better. You could see the sun coming out which meant we had finally made our way to the top. The car rolled over the bump onto its final resting place and we could then see Tony and his man propped up against an old Chevy, waiting.

I searched around for Tommy, but didn't see him so I assumed he must be in the car. Daniel got out of the car first; I stepped right behind him.

"Did you bring the money?" Tony asked, with his condescending laugh.

"Where's Tommy?" I demanded as I showed him the bag.

He nodded toward the strange character next to him. The man then walked toward the back seat of the car and tapped on the window. The darkly tinted window came down and there was my baby still bound and gagged. His face was flush and he looked exhausted from lack of sleep. The man then opened the car door and grabbed Tommy, helping him to stand. They walked back to the spot where the man had been standing and came to rest.

"You walk toward him with the money and he'll walk toward you with the kid," Tony said, confident he was taking control of the situation.

"Guns are planted all around us, ready to fire if anything goes wrong."

I gripped the bag and started walking toward the strange man, but for some reason I felt the need to keep my eyes locked on Tony. It just all seemed a little too easy. I knew Tony still wanted more money and if he didn't have Tommy, there would be nothing left to bargain with.

As I got closer to the strange man, he started to move a little slower, almost like he was hesitating. I slowed down as well; I didn't want to seem too antsy, like an amateur.

Suddenly, like a cat, he reached around and grabbed the money and my arm at the same time. Then he tossed the bag toward Tony and gripped both me and Tommy at the same time. Daniel, without hesitation, bent down and rolled across the concrete toward the man. Shots rang out like the Fourth of July. I grabbed Tommy from the man and held him in my arms. Daniel was right on our heels and the man kicked at his face. Tony was in the car next to the driver and Daniel stood up and punched the driver through the window. Just then, I heard the squealing tires of a second car rounding the corner.

I thought for sure Tony had double-crossed us and the car was coming to kill us, but I was wrong. It was Lucas coming around firing directly at Tony and the driver. Daniel came running at the strange man again but this time he had a gun and it was pointed at my head. Daniel tilted his head at me and I knew exactly what he was thinking. I lowered Tommy down and dropped all my weight on the guy's right side which threw him off balance. Down we went. Daniel was on top of him now and they were fighting. I quickly got up and ran toward the car Lucas was in. I jumped into the back seat with Tommy and removed the blind fold so he could see it was me. As I pulled at it he started to shake horribly so I snatched it quickly and his face lit up with delight when he saw who I was. He buried himself against me I just held on as tight as I could. I heard Tony's cargo screaming by and then Lucas jumped out to help Daniel.

Daniel and Lucas jumped back in and we took off and drove like mad until we were safely home. We ran in the door, locked it and immediately set the alarm. My mom and I took Tommy upstairs to check him out and make sure he wasn't hurt. We were crying and Tommy was laughing. He was so happy to see us I don't think he knew what to do. He had some cuts and bruises, but otherwise he was physically fine. I gave him a bath and dressed him in his pajamas and headed down to get him something to eat. Lucas and Daniel were camped out at the doors with my father pacing around all the windows.

I couldn't help but be extremely happy. I had my son home; he was safe in my arms again and there was nothing else in the world that mattered to me at that moment. I told Lucas I would not be at work the following day because I wanted to be with Tommy and I had to go and visit Chris to let him know what had happened. He agreed and went back to studying the road. Everyone was so distracted by what might happen, but all I knew was I had my son he was right in front of me chowing down on the food I made for him and loving it. He was smiling and laughing and I had the feeling that life again was as it should be other than Chris not being there.

Once everyone had settled down in front of the television, I pulled Lucas aside and asked him to stay the night.

He accepted and asked me what else I had on my mind. Strange how well he knew me. It was almost like he had a link into my mind. I wasn't going to say anything to him until I returned to work but I thought this was as good a time as any.

"I want out," I said. "There's too much at stake and my family isn't worth trading for money. This is the second time Tony has gotten to us and I'm not willing to risk it again."

He looked at me like I had just shot his best friend.

"How can you be shocked?" I asked. "I almost lost my son and my life. I've lost my husband and had to do things he told me I'd never have to do."

Lucas had no choice but to accept my position. The day was filled with tosses and turns and *I* was ready to turn; but it seemed I was the only one.

Mom and dad wanted to get a head start on packing and the guys wanted to stay down stairs and keep a look out for a while longer. I collected Tommy and all the toys he had brought down from his room. We headed upstairs. I stood in the threshold of his bedroom but could not bring myself to put him to bed by himself. He must have felt the same way because he wrapped his arms around my neck and wouldn't let go. I gave in pretty easily and we headed off to my room. I put him down on the bed and he quickly snuggled up to Chris's side along with all his toys. I got dressed and crawled in next to him.

He pushed all his things over and nestled up right next to my arm and held on so tightly it almost broke my heart. I brushed his forehead with my finger and sang to him until he was fast asleep, still clinging on. I scooted down and just stared at him until I fell asleep, too. When I woke up the next morning Tommy wasn't next to me. I panicked and rushed down the hall toward his room but he wasn't there. Running down the stairs, I checked every nook and cranny along the way; he was nowhere in sight. I rested myself against the wall trying to figure out where he might have gone. I knew there was no possible way someone had come into my room in the middle of the night and taken him; but where was he?

I closed my eyes and I could hear him laughing. I squeezed them tighter and I heard it again, but this time it sounded more real. It was sort of faint but also sort of close. I opened my eyes and looked out the window. It was such a sight I had to just stand there and take every part of it in. Out on the swing set in the back yard were my father and my son playing and laughing and having the time of their lives.

Dad was pushing him and giggling while Tommy screamed with delight every time he would swing back. It was such an amazing sight; I just couldn't bring myself to disturb them. I went to the kitchen for coffee instead. My mother was in her usual spot with her coffee, off in her own little world. She looked up and smiled at me and said good morning. I asked her how long those two had been at it and she said all morning. Apparently dad had come upstairs looking for Tommy and panicked when he wasn't in his bed. "The three of them searched the entire house in complete silence trying not to wake you," Mom said. "Once they realized that Tommy was nowhere to be found, your father volunteered to go up and tell you. That's when he discovered the baby had been wrapped up next to you the whole time. Your father ended up sleeping in the chair at the foot of your bed. Tommy woke him up first thing this morning and they have been out there playing ever since."

"It amazes that these men still think that I am so fragile that they have to try and hide every scary thing from me," I said.

My mother put her hand out to stop me.

"Let me tell you something my child, and this is only to be shared between the two of us," she said. "Your father fought with everything he had in him to keep those men from taking that baby. He was mortified to the point that he couldn't face you, feeling that it was his fault your son was taken. If he had disappeared last night, I don't think your father would have made it this time. That's why I think we're better off going home and not knowing what is going on."

I completely understood where she was coming from and I reached over and gave her a huge hug.

My other two protectors came rolling in a little while later saying nothing but reaching over for the coffee. I asked how late they had stayed up and the both responded with, "ugh." Lucas poured his coffee to go and was out the door. Daniel asked what time we were going to see Chris and when we were taking my parents to the airport. I knew that Mom and Dad weren't leaving for a while and I wanted to get in and see Chris, so we went that route.

CHAPTER 12

We sat outside in the waiting room for Chris and he seemed excited to see us. When he saw I wasn't smiling like usual, his face quickly changed. He came around and grabbed us both in a big hug and sat down.

Touching was not permitted but they usually turned an eye to a quick hug. He asked how we were and if everything was all right. I just shook my head no and started to cry. I broke down all the details of the events that had transpired over the last couple of days. He slammed his fist against the table and screamed out. The guard came over and told him to settle down or go back. He apologized and the guard walked away. Chris asked if Tony had been stopped or if he was still out there; I told him the latter.

He told me to have Lucas come to visit with him soon. I agreed and asked that we find another subject to discuss. We talked about the weather and he asked about my parents; we spent an entire hour with small talk until it was time for him to go back. He reminded me to be sure and tell Lucas to come by.

We said our goodbyes and then he was gone again. Each time I went to see him my heart broke a little more. It was almost to the point that I would cringe on the trip there and cry on the trip back. Daniel must have understood my feelings because it seemed to take longer to get there than it did to get back.

Once we got back to the house I noticed that my parents' bags were not by the front door. I called out for my mother and she came out from the kitchen. I explained to her that we really needed to get going or they were going to miss their plane. She shook her head and said that they had changed their minds. She could not live with herself if she left knowing that Chris wasn't home yet. My father also felt that it was his responsibility to take care of me and Tommy while Chris was away. He said Daniel may be the bodyguard, but *he* was the father and would always out rank him. I didn't want to admit it to them but I was so relieved that they were staying. My mother had been such a help with Tommy and every girl needs her father when the times are tough.

Daniel excused himself while we were at dinner and I knew he was going to talk with Lucas again. I wanted to be mad, but at the same time I really didn't want to be involved anymore that I had to. We were in the living room near the end of a movie by the time he came back. He walked through the front door and turned off the alarm.

He asked to speak with me in the kitchen for a moment in private. I followed behind him and noticed a lump in the back of his head. He said that he had been pistol whipped, but didn't want to get into details because he was all right. He and Lucas had just come from a meeting with Tony and some of his men. They came to an agreement, but they were leery of it. Tony had agreed he would no longer come after me or my family, and Lucas let him in on the fact that *he* was the dealer Chris had been working with and any other dealings or problems would have to go through him. I was ecstatic, but afraid all at the same time. I know Tony would have no reason to come after me now that he knew who Lucas was, but he would, of course, be after Lucas full force now. Lucas had only told him to keep Tony away from me and he has also hired an assistant and guard for himself.

The days and nights all seemed to start running together like it was all just one endless day. Lucas was, of course, running full swing with his business. I, on the other hand, seemed to be lacking in a sense. Once the drivers started noticing that Lucas wasn't around as much, they jumped on a fear wagon that I was taking over and the company would go under.

They all came to me, one by one, turning in their resignations and finding other jobs. I was drowning in calls and had no one to run them for me. I called Lucas and he came over right away asking why I hadn't called him before. I knew he was busy and I didn't want to bother him.

"That's ridiculous," he said. "This business is more important to me than anything. I have my whole life and all my savings wrapped up in this company. I can't afford to lose it."

He walked into Chris's office and began making phone calls. Not long after, several of the drivers came walking through the door ready to go back to work. The weeks flew by and the months went by even faster. I had become accustomed to the life I now had without Chris and I wasn't sure how easy it would be to invite him back in.

Chris had an early release hearing coming up in a couple of weeks. His attorney assured us that he would more than likely be released on good behavior. I had convinced myself that I would feel nothing but relief when I heard he was coming home, but now I felt more insecure than ever.

It had been so long since he had been home and a lot had happened. My mother and father had pretty much taken up residence at my house. Daniel and I had become so close, we were completely inseparable, and Lucas has taken total control of the company. Chris was the type of man who wanted control of every aspect of his life. I knew it would be hard for him to get that back.

The drivers were used to reporting to Lucas alone and I wasn't sure if they'd accept Chris the way they used to.

My father put him Chris on a pedestal, but now had a different perspective of him since he hadn't been there when Tommy was abducted. So much would be different and I didn't know how or even if, he would handle it.

As I sat there day dreaming my father came into the room. He had been watching me; for how long, I don't know.

"Where are you," he asked.

"I was off in my own little world having thoughts about what might be," I said, laughing a little.

He nodded and walked away.

The house seemed to be growing by the minute. I felt completely trapped in a tomb and for some reason I just didn't want to be there anymore.

CHAPTER 13

I spoke briefly with my mother and father and they both agreed that a small vacation was in order so I could rest up for Chris's homecoming. We planned to take a drive down to the shore and spend the weekend. We all packed and made final arrangements. It all went more smoothly than I had imagined.

We only lived a couple hours from the beach. The crazy thing was that we had never taken Tommy there before. He was excited. He rode in the back with me and Mom while Daniel and Dad rode up front. Tommy pointed out all the things he had never seen and asked what they were. It was as if my son had not been out of the house since he was born. He wanted to know what everything was and, of course, since I was sitting next to him I had to explain it all.

When we finally arrived at the hotel I was more than willing to go and check us in while everyone else drove around to the room. We went all out on the room, sparing no expense. We got a suite on the top floor overlooking the ocean. There were two adjoining rooms, both were absolutely amazing. Tommy and I shared a suite with Daniel, but there were two separate bedrooms inside. My mother and father shared the other room which only had one bedroom. We had begun to feel relatively safe since Lucas had revealed to Tony exactly who he was. This vacation actually made me feel that I could take some time to relax.

Our days were spent lounging by the pool with big fruity drinks and our evenings were spent walking along the shore and having lavish dinners. It was simply paradise — no phone calls and no one trying to kill us around every corner. I didn't want to leave. I wished that I could stay here forever.

The last night we were there my mother said she felt sleepy and really wasn't up for a walk on the beach. Dad didn't feel up to it either.

They said I could leave Tommy with them and walk alone along the shore, that it would help calm my nerves. Daniel promised to leave a respectable amount of room between us so I could feel that I was alone.

As we made our way along I could feel the warm salty air flowing over me, bringing a sense of peace with it each time. I took my shoes off, rolled up my jeans and ran my feet through the water as I walked. It really was a revitalizing feeling; my mother was right about that. I stopped for a moment and turned to see exactly how far back Daniel was. "I was surprised to find he was almost out of sight. I waved to him to come up and walk with me. I thought this might be a good time to get more information about his family. I knew his parents were both dead, but I didn't know if he had any other family.

"I do have a brother," Daniel said, with a heart-breaking look on his face. "I wouldn't know where to begin to find him."

Our connection was drawn a little closer in that moment. I had never seen any type of emotion from him before. I wasn't sure if he had ever let someone get this close to him before. I put my arm around him and we walked a little farther and then headed back. I never said anything about our conversation to my parents. I wanted him to know he could trust me with.

The next morning as we made our way home, we all looked as if we could have stayed a lot longer. The house was just as we left it; not a single item out of place — it was a nice feeling.

When I got to the office the next morning, Lucas had already beaten me there. He was in Chris's office with the door closed and his obnoxious assistant had planted himself in my chair. He was very much over weight and not too concerned about it. He smelled as if he didn't do laundry and just sprayed all his clothing with air freshener, in addition to the nasty sweat smell. His teeth hadn't met a tooth brush in years. How Lucas decided this man would protect him I wasn't sure. I was normally no so judgmental but there was something about this guy.

I was thankful that Chris had picked my bodyguard instead of Lucas.

"May I have my chair," I politely asked the slob. "I need to get to work."

He apologized and removed his nasty self from my seat. It took all the energy I had not to douse my chair in Lysol right in front of him. I sat there staring at the spreadsheets I had in front of me, but really couldn't concentrate. My mind was on my husband and what life was going to be like when he came home.

Chris had been my whole life for so long that when he was locked up I thought for a time I would cease to exist. Instead, I became independent and totally capable of taking care of myself. I had turned into a completely different woman and I wasn't sure how he would accept me now. What if he wasn't happy with my independence and decided to leave me? I didn't think I could go through losing him twice. What if he decided that he wanted to continue with the illegal stuff, what would become of us then?

I had so many questions and no way to answer them until he came home. Lucas emerged from the office looking as if he had seen a ghost.

"What are you doing here?" Lucas asked. "I didn't know you were back from vacation."

He just shrugged and walked back into the office. His oaf of an assistant followed behind.

I swear if I have to work with that man every day I am going to puke. I mean seriously how disgusting can one human being get?

I knocked on the office door and asked Mr. Nasty to give Lucas and me a moment alone together. He agreed and stepped out, closing the door behind him. I sat in the chair opposite Lucas and asked him seriously where that man had come from. He explained that he had run into the same problem when we hired Daniel. When Lucas told people they would be protecting him from Tony, they refused the position. That man was the only person who would take it.

Lucas admitted the new body guard was gruesome, but said there were no other options.

"What else is going on?" I could tell something else was wrong.

Tony had been sending Lucas death threats, wanting the rest of his money.

"Nothing scary at first, but then this last one came," Lucas said. "He knows I have a brother and knows who he is and he'll go after him if I don't start cooperating."

I didn't know Lucas had any family to speak of, especially someone as close as a brother. He said not to worry that he had everything under control. I left his office and told Daniel I was ready to go home.

I tossed and turned in bed all night thinking of Lucas and his brother. How did Tony know who he was and why did Lucas say it like *he* didn't know. Was it possible that Lucas had a brother out there he doesn't even know?

I remembered the conversation Daniel and I had walking along the beach where he said that he had a brother out there, but he had not seen him in years and jolted straight up, my eyes popping wide open.

What if Daniel and Lucas were brothers and that is why Daniel was here? That would explain why he wanted to stick around so close to us. It would also explain why he wasn't afraid of Tony. If some man was after my brother and his close friends, I would want to be there to protect them. I felt like a private eye figuring out a puzzle.

I am awesome if I do say so myself.

I rested my head back down on my pillow a fell right to sleep. The next morning I came downstairs; Daniel was in the kitchen with my mother and father. They were all laughing about something that I must have missed.

On the ride to the office I decided I would sit up front with Daniel so we could chat. I told him quite confidently that I knew his secret and it was okay for him to tell me that he really did know who his brother was. His jaw dropped and he quickly pulled the car over.

"What are you talking about," Daniel's voice was anxious. "Who do you think my brother is?"

"Lucas, of course," I blurted out. "It all makes sense."

He said there was no way he and Lucas were related. He had seen pictures of both his parents and his brother too.

"Just wishful thinking on my part," I said, embarrassed that I had created the scenario.

How handy would be for me if these two were brothers.

We got to the office Lucas screamed out, "What's up brother?" We both burst out laughing and Lucas was clueless about why.

The next day Lucas was heading out with the driver to Mexico so he could meet with the supplier. Tony had gotten to him and offered him money to stop dealing with Lucas and start working with him. The dealer told Lucas to make Tony go away or he would take him up on his offer.

I felt a little uneasy since this would be the first pay day I was at the office by myself with the drivers. Lucas reassured me that it would all work out and not to worry so much. He waved good-bye and headed off. The drivers came and collected their checks with no a problems.

Lucas had told all of them that he would be out of town and that he had total confidence I could run the place without him. It made me feel good that he believed in me, but awful that I had been with these drivers for so long and still they acted as if they didn't know me. I just chalked it up to being the woman behind the man for so long. Daniel and I ate a wonderful lunch with an eventless afternoon. My life was going good now. Since Lucas had that meeting with Tony, everything had been wonderful.

The next morning Chris had his release hearing, and with Lucas out of town I was extremely busy. I had drivers calling me on my cell phone for pick-up locations and as I stood in front of the courthouse, everyone was screaming at me to be inside. I put my phone on mute and went in. I was being called as a witness for the defense in Chris' case. I would have to stand in front of a judge and convince him that I felt Chris would be better off at home with me. I wasn't sure how I was supposed to make a judge believe it when I wasn't sure I believed it myself? I sat in the back of the small courtroom waiting for my turn to speak. I heard from Marcus's mother who said she would never forgive this man for killing her son. I heard from some of our friends saying that Chris was a model citizen and he didn't deserve to be locked up at all. His attorney was pleading as if he didn't think Chris had a chance in Hell of leaving that place anytime soon. Finally, I was called to come and sit in front of all those people and tell them how badly I wanted my husband to come home.

I sat there in awkward silence for a while trying to figure out the best thing to say. The attorney looked at me and said that I simply needed to tell the truth.

Was he kidding? Did he know that I had these awful feelings deep in the pit of my stomach?

I turned and looked at my husband sitting there vulnerable, waiting for me to speak. I remembered the picture in his office of me when we first met. If our roles were reversed and I was sitting there waiting for him to save me, he wouldn't have hesitated at all. He would have told them what a great person I was, and how much he loved me, and how badly I was needed in the community. So that's what I did. I didn't harp so much on the negative feelings I had inside, but told them about our love and his willingness to help anyone. I went on to tell them about his love for his son and what a great person Chris was. They listened to my words and when I saw the smile Chris had on face, I knew I had done the right thing. I was still in love with him and still had a horrible yearning for him

The judge excused everyone and resigned to his chambers for a brief recess. He would go over all the testimony and come out with a ruling. Chris was moved to a holding cell while we had to wait in the lobby outside of the room. I couldn't see him, or talk to him. Finally, after what seemed like an eternity, the bailiff called us back in. The judge proceeded to have Chris stand up so he could read the findings.

I couldn't bear to watch what was going to happen so I buried my face in my hands. The judge started off by telling Chris that his crime was a heinous one and that he deserved to be punished for it. However, being that he was a model inmate and had so many people willing to stand up for him, he felt that if Chris were to be released there would be no more incidents from him. He granted Chris's an early release and would allow him to go home at the end of the week. I jumped up and screamed, which of course caused the judge to slam his gavel and tell me to contain myself or I would be excused. I apologized and sat back down, but not before giving my husband a little wink. I was so overcome with joy and relief. He was going to be home in a couple of days and all this burden would be lifted. I waved goodbye to him and went back to the office.

Daniel laughed at me. He said he didn't know I had that sort of energy in me. He knew I would be happy about Chris's release, but didn't realize I would get that ecstatic. I just shrugged him off and hurried him along so we wouldn't be any later than we already were.

***

At the office I hit play on the answering machine, but there were no messages. Lucas hadn't called since he left. I checked my cell phone to see if he had tried me there, but again there was nothing. I asked Daniel if he had heard from him — he hadn't.

"It's not like we are brothers," he said, sarcastically.

I just rolled my eyes and turned my attention to the computer screen. I made sure that all the drivers had been dispatched properly since I wasn't exactly taking notes as I sent them out. I took a look at the call log for our Mexico run and it looked like the driver had already called in to say he had arrived. I was still worried about Lucas but decided to believe he got distracted by the meeting and didn't think to call and check in. *I'm not his wife. He doesn't have to check in with me on every move he makes.*

CHAPTER 14

The next couple of days ran like clockwork. Drivers in and out with no problem; the runs were done on time and nothing lacking. Our customers had no complaints and the phones were quiet for the most part. I had wanted to take a couple days off since my husband was coming home, but I hadn't heard from Lucas and didn't know when he planned on returning. I knew this was a bigger shipment, but I hadn't counted on it taking so long to get it back.

As the day wore on, I began to get concerned when the driver's family called to ask where he was. They hadn't heard from him since he left. I called the pick-up point and was told the two men had picked up the waste on time. I called the drop-off and they, too, said the two men were on time for that as well. I started to get that sick feeling in my stomach and I tried the driver's cell phone. I got his voicemail and left a message. I tried Lucas's cell and got his voicemail, too.

I left an urgent message for Lucas hoping he would hear it and get back to me sooner. I was really getting worried. I know he had the meeting with the supplier, but I had no information on him at all.

Maybe Daniel knew more.

He knew who they were, but had no idea on how to get in touch with them. I searched my mind trying to figure how to get in touch with these guys. Then it hit me, the truck they were driving had an anit-theft tracking device. I went to the machine and turned on the tracker. It only took a minute to locate it. It seemed to be stopped and shut down on the side of the road still in Mexico. Daniel was alarmed as well. He recognized the location and knew it was well past the supplier's warehouse. The truck was full of supply and there was no way Lucas, would stop that truck until after he got back to California. Daniel knew something was wrong and immediately picked up his phone and started calling. I told him not to bother trying Lucas's cell because I already had. He just gave me a face and walked into Chris's office, shutting the door behind him.

"Well, he didn't have to be rude about it," I said to myself. "I was only trying to help you Mr. Nasty, but if you're going to be like that than I won't".

I huffed a bit longer and then tried the driver's cell one more time. Again, I got the machine. It was becoming more and more obvious that something was terribly wrong. Daniel was feeling the same way, I could see it in his face. I wondered if he had gotten through to someone he knew who would be willing to go by and check on our truck.

We waited a little while to hear back from his friend and were almost to the point of giving up when his phone rang. The caller told Daniel the truck had been completely abandoned, but there was no trailer hitched to it. That had to be wrong. I had called and they had picked up on scheduled. I asked Daniel if he had any clue as to what was happening. He said he didn't want to raise suspicion, but he believed the trailer had been hijacked. He wasn't sure as to what happened to our men, but he wanted to head down there and find out. He wanted to make some private calls and to make arrangements for the trip so he went to Chris's office where he could use the phone. I tried to survey all the information to see if I could make sense of anything, but I couldn't. There was no possible way anyone could have known what that truck was doing other than delivering hazardous material.

Who would want to steal a trailer like that? Who would even want to go near a trailer like that?

Daniel was on the phone in Chris's office and I really wanted to hear what he was saying. I tiptoed very quietly to get closer to the door so I might be able to hear him. I walked closer and closer and finally reached the door. I slowly pressed my ear up to it just like on a movie; it always seems to work on TV. I had a hard time making out exactly what he was saying, but it seemed he was on the phone with an airline scheduling a flight, which meant I missed the juicy stuff.

As I turned to head back to my desk, my telephone started ringing. I bolted across the room and did a quick spin around in my chair. I answered the phone with the normal, "Thank you for calling," intro. All I heard for the first couple of seconds was heavy breathing, then a sort of whopping sound in the back ground. Finally, I heard the voice of my driver asking if I was alone. I was so relieved to hear from him I started asking a million questions, but he quickly interrupted me. I caught onto the fact that his tone was full of fear and he wasn't calling to check in. He asked again if I was alone. I told him that I was here with Daniel, but no one else. Then another voice came on the phone and when he spoke, my heart sunk down in my chest. It was Tony – he was enraged.

"I am through playing games, I told you once that I wasn't going to give up until I got everything I was due and I meant it," Tony yelled. "Now I have your trailer and I have your men. I tried to do this peacefully, but you all wouldn't cooperate so now I have no choice. I am going to take this trailer and give it to the police unless you give me the money that it's worth."

Daniel had come into the room and I held the phone out for both of us to hear. He grabbed the receiver and told Tony he would do whatever he asked as long as he promised not to harm Lucas or our driver. Tony said he wasn't making any promises anymore, because he was tired of getting double crossed. He also said that if it came down to it, he would kill every last one of us. He gave us 48 hours to come up with the cash he had been asking for or he was taking the trailer and the men to the police station in Mexico.

I wasn't a criminal, but even I knew the prisons in Mexico are ten times worse than the ones here. The problem we had was all of the business accounts were in Lucas's and Chris's name. I had no way of getting that kind of money.

Daniel stopped me, "We're not giving Tony a dime." He was going to get that trailer and those men and then he would give Tony what he should have a long time ago.

"You're nuts," I said. "If the police get a hold of any of our information then we are all done for, including me. I'm not willing to go to jail for something I got out of a long time ago."

"Go home," Daniel said calmly. "I'll let you know when the situation has been handled. Don't worry."

I hadn't driven a car in forever, but Daniel insisted that I needed to go home alone. He was going to get a cab to the airport. My instructions were to get in the car and go straight home, not stopping anywhere — go inside, lock the door and turn on the alarm. Tommy and I were to stay that way until I heard from Daniel.

As I approached the first light it was red. I pulled to a stop. Out of nowhere a man pulled open my door and snatched me out of the car. He put a cloth to my face and I blacked out.

When I came to, my head hurt so badly I could barely open my eyes. I could tell I was in some sort of chair and it was very hard. I pushed my feet around and was relieved I could touch the ground. I heard Tony's voice trying to get me to open my eyes. The pain subsided enough that I could squint, and then open a bit. I could see two men I didn't recognize and Tony.

Well this is great. I thought to myself. I have been kidnapped by this lunatic again.

As I opened my eyes a bit wider I could see Lucas. He was beaten up pretty badly. Next to him was the driver. He was bruised up as well.

How on Earth did I get to Mexico and where is Daniel?

Tony began telling me that he never had any intention of going to the police. He just wanted to make sure Daniel and I separated so he could get to me. He said Daniel had fooled him once, but there was no way he was going to let that happen again.

I caught a glimpse of Daniel running by but made sure no one saw my eyes following him. Tony was going on about what he was going to do and how we were all going to suffer for the pain we caused him.

A net fell from the ceiling and it landed over everyone but Tony, including Lucas and the driver. Tony started shooting at the ceiling. I tried to get loose from the chair. I must not have been tied too tight because my hands broke free easily. I reached down and untied my legs and hid behind the chair. Tony was still shooting at the ceiling while the other men were trying to get free from the net. I crawled around to where Lucas and the driver were and tried to help them, but Tony's guys were grabbing at me. I just ran.

Daniel was right around the corner and he showed me the way to get out — told me to run to the nearest station hide. Tony was right behind him and before Daniel could turn around to defend himself, Tony pistol whipped him to the ground. I was already to the exit before Tony started screaming for me and shooting. I quickly ducked out the door and ran as fast as I could. Once I realized Tony wasn't following me, I knew I had to go back and help Daniel or they were all going to die.

I ran back toward the building and pushed my body up against the wall outside the exit door. I stood and listened to see if anyone was coming and heard nothing. Tony must have assumed I was long gone and was going back to take care of business. I tiptoed my way down the hallway and stood outside the door to the warehouse were they all were. Tony had Daniel down on the ground, kicking, hitting and beating the crap out of him. Finally, Daniel reached his hand up as if to tell him he wanted to say something.

Tony stopped and pulled him up to a seated position. Daniel turned his head to the side and spit out a bunch of blood. Then, he turned to Tony.

"You know for years I searched trying to find the person I had spent my childhood with," Daniel said. "Then one day I saw a picture of you in the paper and I knew it was you. I wasn't completely positive so I decided to come here and try to get to know you a little better — do some digging so I could know for sure. When I got to your little town it seemed that everyone around here hated you and I thought, naw, it couldn't be him. I took a job to get close to you to try and better understand who you were. I got your medical history pinpointed it down to the birth date, and that is when I knew. The only question I have is why brother, why would you go from being such a great big brother to such a horrible human being?"

I was completely stunned. He had to be wrong.

I noticed the stairs leading up to the balcony above Tony's head so I went up.

I looked around for something I could use to disarm Tony, but there was nothing up there but lint. I saw a rope draped over the side. It was connected to the other side of the building. I knew that I was probably going to die, especially if the rope wouldn't hold me. There was no telling how old the rope was and if it was still attached on the other side. I didn't have time to be concerned. I sucked up my fear and grabbed a hold of the rope.

I crawled over the ledge and wrapped the rope around my waist. I grabbed a hold of the end of the rope and jumped out. I flew across the warehouse and nearly threw up. I had too much adrenalin and determination to stop now, so I pushed all my weight forward so I could go faster. Daniel must have seen me coming because he ducked down which made Tony turn to see what he was hiding from. I smacked right into Tony full force and knocked us both down on the ground. Without a second thought I rolled over and grabbed his gun and pointed it at him. He held his hands up and Daniel quickly went to get Lucas and the driver loose. Daniel grabbed the rope I had swung down with and cut a part of it off. He sat Tony down in the chair and tied the rope around him. We all took off and jumped in the truck Tony had attached to our trailer.

We had no idea what condition the cargo was in, but we knew we needed to be far away before we could inventory it. We drove for a long time. I could tell from driver's face that he would be leaving us the second we reached California. I honestly couldn't blame him. Once we felt we were far enough away we pulled off at a rest area and pulled open the back to survey the damage. Everything seemed to be all right, nothing had been touched at all. I guess Tony thought he was just going to take the whole lot and do with it what he pleased. I quickly phoned my mother to check on Tommy and to let her know that we were all okay.

Daniel grabbed the phone and told her to get them all out of the house and to go somewhere safe until we could get there. He didn't want Tony to be able to get to them. He told Mom to take her phone and we would contact her and give a special code to let her know that everything was good.

"Don't move until you hear that code," he yelled to stress his point.

Daniel knew we couldn't stay in one place for too long. It wouldn't have taken Tony long to get loose and come after us.

***

Gunshots rang out around us and we could see a car coming right at us.

"This man is relentless," I said to Daniel. "I swear I am going to stand here and shoot him just so we don't have to deal with him anymore."

Daniel grabbed my arm and threw me in the truck. We were driving and they were shooting. I felt like I had been transported into one of the horrible action movies Chris used to watch all the time.

Then I saw it. A bullet shot right through my hair and into Daniel's arm. I screamed and Lucas told me to grab the gun there was no time. He told me I had to shoot out the tires or they were going to have the advantage over us. I stuck my head out the window and aimed my gun. I aimed it right at the front tire and I shot. The car swerved and then flew off the road. BAMM, it exploded.

I turned back in the truck and sat up right in the seat. I turned toward Lucas who was staring at me as if for the first time. He never said a word. As we rode along in silence it hit me, I had finally gotten my revenge. Finally, after all this time I was rid of the man who had caused so much harm and grief for my family.

The morning was full of sunshine and warmth. As I stood there I went over the events of the last several days in my mind.

How had I gone from being this meek little house wife, to a mobster sharp shooter in such a short amount of time?

Tommy yanked at my shirt and started pointing. There he was, the man of my dreams, running toward us as they opened the large barbed wire gates. I picked Tommy up and we ran toward him, meeting somewhere in the middle. Chris scooped us up in a big hug and we just stood there for a moment trying to savor every second of the embrace. He put his arm around me and we walked to the car. Daniel was standing by the car, his arm still in a sling.

"What happened to you my brother?" Chris asked. "Oh nothing much, just a run in with an old enemy. Not to worry though he won't be meddling around here anymore."

Chris hugged him, patted him on the back and we headed home.

Later I pulled Daniel to the side and asked him why he didn't say anything about what had happened.

"Listen, what happens in Mexico, stays in Mexico and that's all there is."

***

Lucas and Chris went back to work as usual, but this time there was no side job. Lucas gave up the drug game and went with simply being a legitimate business man.

My parents reluctantly went back home and life was starting to be normal again. It didn't take long for Chris to make his way back to the top, being the charming man that he is. Daniel was asked to stay on at the company not as a body guard, but as a third partner in the business.

He got his own house and started to live his own life. The fairy-tale life I had dreamed of for so long was unfolding before my eyes. All it took was nearly losing everything.

My husband tells me that I changed while he was away. He has no idea how right he is.

ABOUT THE AUTHOR

Robin Boren resides in Louisville, Kentucky with her husband and three beautiful daughters.

Visit her Web site at www.robinboren.moonfruit.com

WWW.MARTINSISTERSPUBLISHING.COM

www.ingramcontent.com/pod-product-compliance
Lightning Source LLC
Chambersburg PA
CBHW071405170626
46811CB00003B/1264